METEOR

DAYS OF ANARCHY

J.D. MARTENS

EPIC Escape

An Imprint of EPIC Press
abdopublishing.com

Days of Anarchy
The Meteor: Book #2

Written by J.D. Martens

Copyright © 2018 by Abdo Consulting Group, Inc.

Published by EPIC Press™
PO Box 398166
Minneapolis, MN 55439

All rights reserved.

Printed in the United States of America.

International copyrights reserved in all countries.
No part of this book may be reproduced in any form without
written permission from the publisher. EPIC Press™ is trademark
and logo of Abdo Consulting Group, Inc.

Cover design by Candice Keimig
Images for cover art obtained from iStock
Edited by Amy Waeschle

LIBRARY OF CONGRESS CATALOGING-IN-PUBLICATION DATA
Names: Martens, J.D., author.
Title: Days of anarchy/ by J.D. Martens
Description: Minneapolis, MN : EPIC Press, 2018 | Series: The Meteor; #2
Summary: Jeremy and his friends drive to Vail to escape possible rioting and anarchy after the
    United States reveals the truth about the comet. As the discontent continues on the ground,
    Dr. Miller and Dr. Lahdka grapple with the ramifications of failure, while Jeremy searches
    for meaning in a new world. Meanwhile, something is afoot in the Rocky Mountains.
Identifiers: LCCN 2017946136 | ISBN 9781680768282 (lib. bdg.)
    | ISBN 9781680768565 (ebook)
Subjects: LCSH: Adventure stories—Fiction. | End of the world—Fiction.
    | Meteor showers—Fiction. | Teenagers—Fiction | Young adult fiction.
Classification: DDC [FIC]—dc23
LC record available at http://lccn.loc.gov/2017946136

For my lovely niece, Avery—my inspiration comes from you.

1

AN INDIAN GOD AND A HOTEL IN DALLAS

June 18, 2016
Near Corsicana, Texas

"Let's get some gas. Also, I need to pee," Anna yawned, looking out the window.

Jeremy, Anna, Dustin, and Karina were an hour south of Dallas in Dustin's Acura, speeding up Interstate 45. Their backs clung to the leather of their seats and the car's air was thick and humid. Since Jeremy wanted to save gas, they didn't use the air conditioner. It was fourteen hours after President Chaplin had announced to the world that a rather large frozen rock—a comet nicknamed Shiva—would probably hit the Earth in around two years. At the last gas station they had gone to—an unassuming Chevron outside of Houston—they had almost been shot, so when Anna suggested they go to the next gas station, Jeremy refused.

"Just pee in one of those Gatorade bottles," Jeremy said, keeping his eyes on the road.

"Are you kidding me?" Karina exclaimed.

"Jer, I can't do that," Anna sighed, before continuing, "I don't want to go to another gas station any more than you do, but we have to. We don't have a choice. We need gas."

"We have some gas in the U-Haul, in the gas canisters," Jeremy reasoned.

"And when we run out of that? I am not so sure my mom's Triple-A card is going to work in Anarch-Merica," Dustin remarked. "Sooner or later, we are going to need gas."

"Stop calling it that, Dustin," Jeremy said, but the others grinned.

Jeremy knew they were right, of course, and saw they were approaching a Shell station, so they went over their attack plan. If there were more than two cars there, they would drive to another gas station. Everyone would stay in the car except Dustin, who sat closest to the gas tank flap. He would jump out and pump the gas, and then get back into the car and wait for it to be done. Once he heard the click of the full gas tank, he'd jump out again, pull out the pump, screw the lid back on the tank, and get in the car. Anna would not pee, and instead at some point they would stop somewhere they knew was safe and where there were no people. They would talk to no one, and everything would run smoothly.

"I heard a saying once from my Greek exchange student," Dustin said. "'When you make plans, God laughs.'"

"God must be laughing pretty hard, then," Karina said, looking up at the sky.

When the Shell came into view, they were all thankful to see only one car there. The entire gas station was otherwise deserted. Dustin hopped out of the car, but immediately stuck his head back in through the door.

"It says cash only. What should we do?"

You want something done, you gotta do it yourself, Jeremy thought, and opened the door.

"You take the wheel," he said to Dustin as he stepped out of the car.

"Jer, what about the buddy system?" Anna asked, worried.

Jeremy walked toward the gas station, nervously stroking what stubble his chin had been able to grow. He stepped into the small store, looking around, and saw a thickly mustached man staring at him.

"Oh, hello," Jeremy said.

"What do you want?" the man asked, sternly but not unfriendly.

Jeremy looked nervously at the handgun the man held. He had his hand on the handle, and it was pointed at Jeremy, but his finger was not yet on the trigger. The man saw Jeremy eyeing the handgun.

"Don't be nervous, boy, just taking precaution. Got robbed here this morning, since the world is gonna end and all."

"Right," Jeremy said tensely. "Can I get a full tank on two and some chips?"

The man nodded, and pressed some numbers on the computer to his left, while keeping his eyes on Jeremy. Jeremy, meanwhile, was sure to keep his hands in plain view of the man. He didn't want the guy thinking he was going to do anything wrong.

"That'll be two-hundred dollars, even," the man said.

"What? Are you joking?" Jeremy had $220 in his pocket, but he couldn't believe the guy wanted that much.

"Desperate times, I can charge whatever I want." The man angled the gun to point at Jeremy's heart.

Jeremy looked to the old man and narrowed his eyes distrustfully, and gave the man the money, taking a bag of chips on his way out. His wallet felt much lighter. He walked back to the car and began pumping the gas, and his phone buzzed. It was a text from his dad.

I'm sorry for how we left things, son. I hope you'll let me

know you're safe and I look forward to hearing from you. Be careful. Things are already changing in Houston.

Jeremy thought for a moment about how to respond, his thumbs hovering over the keyboard, but his mind came up empty. *I'll respond later,* he thought.

As Jeremy drove through Dallas, he saw people swerving all over the road. Many people held guns in their cars. There were preachers on the side of the road, raving about the coming apocalypse.

Anna suggested that the credit cards might stop working soon, so they should use them while they could. She thought they should stay at the Ritz Carlton in downtown Dallas, and Dustin eagerly agreed, having never stayed at a hotel like that before.

"Are you guys sure we should do this? I mean, we could be getting ourselves into trouble. It might be better to just drive and sleep away from people who might try to kill us," Jeremy said, thinking about their two gas station encounters. Jeremy had almost gotten his friends killed at their first stop because he hesitated at the pump. If that man had raised his gun just a little higher, he could have shot Anna, but luckily the bullet just went into the car door.

"I think Jeremy's right," Karina said. "What if someone tries to steal our car or our stuff or something?"

"It might happen, guys," Dustin mentioned. "But think of it this way. It's getting dark soon, and there will be people on the road who want to do us harm too. If we are in a hotel room, what could happen? We can lock the door, and we have four people."

Anna spoke up. "We can't think that everyone is out to get us."

"I don't agree. Everyone *is* probably out to get us!" Karina retorted.

They couldn't agree; it was a two–two vote. Dustin said that since it was split down the middle in a vote, they should flip a coin.

"Heads," Jeremy said, and held his breath.

Dustin had a big grin on his face as the coin flipped in the air and landed on his palm . . . It was tails!

"This is such a dumb idea," Jeremy bemoaned. "Someone literally tried to kill us for this car, and you want to go into a big city where guns are legal?"

But Jeremy was voted down, and they got off the freeway. On the streets of Dallas they saw people walking around the city, fully armed and dangerous. *How could we be so stupid?* Jeremy thought.

Jeremy bit his nails as Dustin drove into the roundabout for the Ritz Carlton Dallas. The dual flags of the United States and Texas jutted out of the tall building, and incredibly the valet stood professionally at his post, despite the president's address the day before. At first they considered giving the car to the valet, but Jeremy convinced them that they couldn't possibly be thinking of giving the keys to their "apocalypse car" to a kid their same age. They parked it in the self-parking lot, which took a while because they needed an extra spot for the U-Haul.

The group walked into the Ritz and it was beautiful. There were great oak columns on the edges of the lobby, ornate mirrors on the walls, and a beautiful chandelier hung above them. Jeremy eyed the luxurious lobby suspiciously, expecting someone to pop out at any moment and attack them.

"Hello!" Dustin said eagerly to the cute and bored-looking clerk named Sheila. "We would like to rent your most expensive room, please. Whatever the honeymoon suite is, we'll take that!"

Dustin winked and threw his arm around Karina, who affected a smile while trying her very best not to roll her eyes.

"That suite is eight thousand dollars, sir," Sheila replied calmly.

"No problem, Sheila," Dustin answered, handing her a credit card.

After a minute or so of Dustin looking at Karina to keep up the appearance of their engagement, and Karina awkwardly trying to avoid Dustin's gaze, Sheila gave Dustin the card back.

"I'm afraid it's been declined. I think that price is over the daily limit of your credit card, sir."

"Oh," Dustin replied, unsure of what to do next.

They tried a few more cards, but it didn't work. Eventually they settled on the lower suite, the "Ritz-Carlton Suite." It was only four-thousand dollars. Jeremy thought the entire exchange was suspicious. *Why would she be working even after the President Chaplin speech about the comet?* he wondered.

Together the group walked with their backpacks of essentials and got into the elevator.

Dustin had to insert a key into the elevator so he could even click the "8th floor" button.

"Wow," Dustin began. "You can't even get to this floor without a special key."

They walked past the hotel rooms in the hallway until they reached a room at the end of the wing. The entrance of the room said "Ritz-Carlton Suite" on it and there were two doors instead of one. *Maybe this is a good idea,* Jeremy thought.

Dustin stuck the room key in the slot, and as they entered the room, the girls gasped. Jeremy held his breath, and Dustin walked in with his mouth agape. Jeremy saw the dining room table with a unique-looking art piece in the middle of it. It looked like an elegant branch of an oak tree, deeply stained an earthy color. Straight ahead were enormous double windows, which looked over the Dallas skyline. In front of the huge windows was a glass coffee table with ornate couches surrounding it, facing an impossibly thin TV.

Jeremy went and sat down next to it, turning it on. Anna locked the deadbolt to the room, and slid the chain-lock over as a second security measure. Dustin ran and jumped on the California King in the master bedroom. "Dibs!" he laughed.

Jeremy watched as the "Ritz Carlton" logo danced across the screen before CNN came on the screen, and a pundit began speaking about the day's events. Karina turned on the rainforest shower in the bathroom and closed the door.

"The president is about to speak again . . . " Jeremy said, continuing to stare at the TV. The news ticker was scrolling along, repeating the words "State of

Emergency in West Coast cities . . . San Francisco, Seattle . . . "

"What exactly does that mean?" Dustin asked Jeremy, reading the news ticker.

"It means that enough people weren't obeying the regular laws, as we saw while we drove to Dallas, only worse. Maybe they'll declare martial law soon."

"And give the military more power? That's not good."

"Maybe fewer people will try to shoot us if they think the military might come after them if they break the law."

"Maybe . . . "

Even though they had just started their journey, Jeremy sank deeply into the Ritz-Carlton couch, unable to keep his eyes open for long.

• • •

Robert Miller had assembled his team, packed his belongings, and sat in the back of the military

Humvee, watching the flat Texan landscape whiz by. Suri Lahdka, his trusted coworker—and now probably his best friend—sat next to him. They went over the team they had assembled together, complete with new engineers and scientists. They were to go to the National Laboratory, which was in Los Alamos. Robert couldn't believe that seventy years ago J. Robert Oppenheimer made the journey to Los Alamos to make the world's first atomic bomb, and now he and Suri were heading there to send nuclear weapons into space.

Robert stared ahead before turning to Suri, saying, "It's crazy to think that the same technology that almost destroyed the world might save it now."

Suri nodded. "At least we aren't building the bomb. We are just trying to blow up a really big rock."

Just then, Robert's phone rang.

"Robert Miller," Robert spoke into his phone.

A peculiar accent replied, saying, "Dr. Miller, this is Gerald Jan. I believe we spoke around a month ago. I called myself Mr. S."

Robert quietly put Gerald on speakerphone, putting his finger to his mouth to Suri, who nodded.

"Right, Gerald, how can I help you?"

"I was hoping you would come to Hawthorne, California, to my factory. I have something I want to show you."

"Actually, Gerald, I'm sure you're aware of what I do and you may know, somehow, that I'm on my way to an undisclosed location—"

"You're on your way to Los Alamos. Listen, Doctor, I have the world's best programmers and hackers working for me. Please come. I want to show you what I've built. I think that it will come in handy. This is a conflict that will obviously affect us all, and I want the next generation to survive. I will pay whatever it costs to get you over here."

Robert looked over at Suri, who gracefully reached over and tapped the "mute" button on Robert's phone.

Suri looked thoughtful, and said, "I think we should go. I mean, Gerald might have an unconventional way of doing things, but he's really big in the tech sphere. He's been building a lot of rockets at SpaceX, and he knows how important this is. He wouldn't ask you to go out of your way if it wasn't something extremely important."

"He does seem a little self-important though," Robert mused.

Suri raised her eyebrows. "You know that saying about the pot and the kettle?"

Robert laughed, ignoring the quip. "The guy does seem smart. Let's do it. Mr. Jan? Are you there?"

Suri reached over and unmuted Robert's phone for him and Robert tried again. "Mr. Jan, tell me where to go and I'd be happy to meet you."

"You're on your way to a military plane, correct?"

"Yes."

"Well, tell the pilot you need to make a stop at Vandenberg Airforce Base, in California. I'll be waiting here with Vishnu."

"Vishnu?!" Suri exclaimed, rolling her eyes in exasperation. *Another Hindu name?!* she thought.

"Hello, Miss Ladhka. I didn't realize you were there as well. Yes, I've nicknamed my invention Vishnu, because I figured we should stay constant with the Indian gods."

Robert couldn't hide his smile as he said goodbye to Gerald Jan, telling him he would reach Vandenberg in around three and a half hours.

Once they reached the air field, Robert spent fifteen minutes convincing the pilot to stop in California. Finally the pilot conceded that Robert—since, after all, he was in charge of saving the world—should be allowed to make a detour if he thought it was appropriate and relevant to his plan to stop Shiva.

2

INTIMACY

July 19, 2016
Downtown Dallas

Jeremy woke up groggily on the pullout couch. It was difficult to pull himself away from Anna's grasp, who held him tightly. Sometimes being under blankets with someone you love feels more secure than a bulletproof vest. There was another knock at the door.

"Who is it?" Jeremy asked, but no one answered.

He peered through the peephole, but saw no one.

"Should I open it?" he posed, to no one in particular.

Anna had drifted back to sleep, and muttered something that sounded a lot like, "Yes . . . no." Jeremy decided to ignore the last part.

He opened the door slowly with the door-chain still attached, peering out.

"Hello?"

Again, no one answered, but he looked down and saw a newspaper on the floor. It was the *USA Today*.

He swiped it up, closed the door, and turned on the coffee in the room. Four-thousand dollars a night, but at least they gave you free coffee. Jeremy wondered why the Ritz-Carlton employees seemed to have maintained their professionalism. Going to work after learning about Earth's expiration date—commitment indeed!

Jeremy looked down at the newspaper in his hands. The headline blared: "Martial Law in California, Washington State."

Jeremy read a list of bullet points which told the citizens their new laws. "In these states where President Chaplin has instituted Martial Law, the military has been granted permission to search any civilian, confiscate goods in service of the State . . . "

Jeremy was interrupted by a buzzing sensation in his pocket. It was a text from his dad.

Jeremy. Please come home—your mother is worried about you.

Jeremy texted back. I'm doing fine, Dad. Don't worry about me. I'm going to stay up north for a while. I'll tell you when we get to Vail.

Jeremy felt guilty for running away, but he was just doing it to be safe, and his friends needed him. His parents would not have come with him even if he had asked them to go sooner, and at the same time he thought they would be relatively safe. Anyone who took power would want to make use of his Dad's contracting abilities. For now, Jeremy put it out of his mind. *At least my parents won't have to worry about me*, he thought.

Jeremy walked over to the master bedroom and knocked on the door.

"Hey, we should get going, alright? Let's leave in ten minutes."

"Sure," a muffled voice replied.

Jeremy took a shower and woke up Anna. Jeremy turned on the television and saw aerial footage of San Francisco. He could see the streets burning.

"What's going on?" Anna asked, blinking at the TV.

Jeremy turned the volume up. A reporter was speaking. ". . . the West Coast. San Francisco is now the center of anarchy. The military has been forced north of Golden Gate Bridge. They've been cut off south of the airport. It is unclear what is going on in San Francisco at this moment. For those of you just tuning in, San Francisco has fallen. San Francisco has fallen. I'm also getting word right now that Utah, in conjunction with the Mormon Church, has shut its borders.

"Whoa . . . " Jeremy said.

"Yeah . . . " Anna gasped, unable to think of anything else to say.

Jeremy looked at his friends' horrified faces.

The reporter continued. "The rockets that have been leaving Cape Canaveral and Southern California and Alaska are not all observation satellites, but in fact are nuclear weapons aimed to move the meteor off its course."

"Didn't Dr. Miller say it was a comet?" Anna asked, looking up at Jeremy.

"Shh."

"We've been given word that they have all been working as planned, and should reach the meteor in two months' time. The question remains: with NASA's shaky history, who's to say those bombs will reach the meteor? Who's to say some of them won't fail, and descend back onto our country? Jacksonville, North Carolina, considered by some to be the 'buckle' of the Bible belt, along with many prominent Southern Baptist preachers, have mentioned that the coming meteor is not a coincidence, but that the meteor coming toward Earth is in fact the work of divine intervention. It did not come from deep space; it came from God Almighty. God is coming, and He is mad. He is coming as He did in Noah's time, and is going to wipe out the sinners from the world, and bring those of us who have led pious lives to Heaven."

Anna shut off the TV. "We don't need to listen to this nonsense," she said.

Dustin sat with his phone in his lap, reading the NASA press release issued just after President Chaplin's speech.

"He isn't even right," Dustin remarked. "The reporter said that it came from outside the solar system, but it actually came from the Kuiper Belt. He's not even right about that."

Jeremy looked behind the couch, where Karina was staring at the TV, a tear rolling down her cheek.

"Are you okay?" Jeremy asked.

Karina didn't answer, walked past them briskly, and sat down in the other room.

"What's up with her?" Jeremy whispered to Anna.

"She's a pretty strict Christian. Her family went to an Evangelical church. I remember she used to tell me stories from the Bible when we had sleepovers. Stories about Noah and stuff."

"You don't think she actually thinks that Judgement Day is coming, do you?"

"I don't know, it's hard to say. I'm not saying that God picked up a rock and threw it toward Earth, but maybe he influenced the meteo—comet in some unknown way," Anna said, deep in thought. "If the comet does actually hit us and we all die, that's just it?"

"What do you mean?" Jeremy asked Anna.

"I mean, if we all die, what do you think will happen to everyone on Earth? All our . . . souls?"

"Nothing," Jeremy said quickly. "I think it'll all just end."

"That's sad."

"Yeah, I guess it is . . . " Jeremy said.

Jeremy packed his bags while the others did the same, and they got ready to leave. The group walked down the hallway and clicked the button for the lobby. Jeremy looked over at Karina, who seemed to have recovered from what she'd seen on television. When the elevator doors slowly opened, there was no one in sight. The receptionist post was empty, and there was an eerie air in the building. To Jeremy it felt like the air was thick, like flowers would wilt faster if they were breathing this air too long.

Suddenly, Karina spoke up and stared at Anna. "I have to go to the bathroom."

It took her a second to understand, but then she quickly replied, "Oh, I'll go with you!"

Jeremy and Dustin then waited for them outside the girls' bathroom.

"What was that all about?" Jeremy asked.

"Karina and I made out last night," Dustin said excitedly.

"Really?"

"Yeah, man, but it was weird. You guys were asleep on the pullout and I was in the shower, and I just got out, and Karina was lying on that big bed. I don't know where she came from. Then we started cuddling, and then . . . you know . . . And after she was super upset, like a different person than before."

"What do you mean?"

"She kept on crossing her heart like the Catholics do, and saying, 'It's coming,' over and over again."

"I don't know, man . . . " Jeremy replied, unsure of what to make of it either.

"They're probably talking about it right now in the bathroom," Dustin murmured.

"Oh, that's definitely what they're doing," Jeremy laughed.

Dustin punched Jeremy in the arm, and then they were quiet for a while. The total quietness of the hotel was very evident, and their steps created an eerie echo in the marble lobby.

The girls came out of the bathroom, and the walk to the car was a bit awkward, but before long they were talking and joking around again, driving out of Dallas. Oddly, they did not see anyone on the roads, but since they had woken up so early perhaps this was normal. They made sure to drive around Fort Worth, thinking it might be better to avoid major cities.

Anna took the wheel to start, with Karina as the navigator.

Meanwhile, two hundred miles away, Robert's daughter Jennifer, whom Robert had asked Jeremy to take care of and check in on, was also driving with her husband and daughter toward the Rocky Mountains. A map of the Rocky Mountains lay open on Jennifer's lap. Jeremy's number was scribbled in the top right corner with "For Emergencies" written under it.

• • •

"It's magnificent!" Robert gasped, gazing in wonder at Gerald Jan's spaceship.

"This can escape Earth's orbit?" Suri asked.

"When it's ready," Gerald said, his arms folded, looking up proudly at Vishnu.

Robert stood on the factory floor of SpaceX's largest facility in Hawthorne, California, next to Suri and Mr. Jan. The factory was enormous. At four stories tall, it looked three times the size of a Costco. Every five minutes or so a worker would run up to Gerald and rattle off some numbers, at which point

Gerald would nod or make a quick comment. Then the worker would scribble something down on his clipboard and scurry off.

Robert looked in awe at the huge spaceship that Mr. Jan had built with the help of his team at SpaceX. It looked like a gigantic metal egg lined with bulb-like protuberances that looked like tumors. There were rows of these little tumors going up the craft. This hulking mass reminded Robert of some of the more unpleasant-looking inventions of the age—like the Honda Element, or those hats that held beer cans.

"It's designed to orbit the comet, with a lot of three-dimensional maneuverability," Gerald began. "What I'm hoping is that these little bumps, the bulbs, are places where we can affix nuclear bombs, which can shoot down at Shiva with devastating accuracy, and with a real-time effectiveness. And the best part is that this ship will be manned."

"Seriously?" Suri asked, astonished.

"Oh, it's not nearly done, but since the ship will

orbit the comet, it will be one of our best weapons in widening the gaseous jets."

"It looks like it'll be difficult to maneuver her though," Robert commented. "She'll need a lot of flexibility in motion."

"Exactly. She's pretty heavy, but up in space we'll make good use of the reverse thrusters to get her into orbit with the comet. We learned a lot from the European Space Agency's Rosetta Satellite. Vishnu can act as both a vessel from where we can launch bombs, and a way to maintain a close visual on the comet as it comes closer to Earth."

Gerald looked clean and was dressed in a simple black T-shirt, belt, and khaki pants. For someone who hadn't grown up in the tech revolution, seeing Gerald Jan in the flesh was not particularly awe-inspiring for Robert, who saw him as another billionaire entrepreneur. But to Suri it felt like she was meeting the President of the United States—which was saying something considering she'd already done that. Gerald was the man that all her friends at MIT idolized—the tech "god" who taught them to work harder than anyone else, be creative, and never stop innovating.

"When is your launch date?"

Suri had to admit that the spaceship was aptly named. Vishnu was known as the "preserver" or "protector," one of Hinduism's three major gods. Considering Comet J312 was nicknamed Shiva, the "destroyer," it made sense that this hefty nuclear bomb gun named Vishnu would act as Preserver of Earth.

Robert walked around, and for the next few hours they discussed the efficacy of Vishnu's use. Sending a manned ship to orbit Earth was something that Robert and Suri had briefly considered, but given the speed at which they needed to begin bombing the comet, it was more efficient to simply begin making single-use nuclear missiles. Yet having Vishnu would definitely help. Robert thought that perhaps having Gerald working alongside them was a good idea, even if it meant he'd be farther away from his factory.

"Gerald, would you like to come work with us?" Robert asked.

Gerald thought for a moment, never uncrossing his arms. Suri checked her phone and saw her mom was calling. Embarrassed, she excused herself.

"Hi, Mom, what's up?"

"Hi, Suri, did you make it to Los Alamos?"

"Actually we made a stop in Los Angeles for a little research."

"Okay, honey. Well, be careful. I think the president could declare Martial Law soon, so the civil rights we have would pretty much go away. You know what they do to minorities if the military gains control, right?"

Suri tried ignoring her mother's paranoia, and responded, "Just be careful, Mom. I don't know what's going to happen either."

"I need to tell you—it's amazing what you're doing, Suri, but I think we would feel more comfortable in India. You know . . . if the world really does end."

"What? *Maaji,*" Suri replied aghast, using the

Hindi word for mother. "Are you serious? You're going back to India? Are flights even operating?"

"We bought tickets with a whole group of Indians and found a pilot who will take us. We just think it will be safer. Here we have all these people who think there's going to be some 'Judgment Day.' And that name . . . Shiva. I fear these people may start to blame Indians for this. And, of course, everyone has guns here, Suri. Did you know that?"

Suri replied dryly, "Yes, *Maaji*, I know, it's crazy . . ."

"You'll try to come visit us? And if you can't—" Suri's mother began to choke up, and Suri was having trouble hearing her.

"You know I won't be able to visit you," Suri explained. "There's still so much to do."

Robert looked over in Suri's direction and saw her crying. He excused himself from Gerald.

"Hey, why don't you go back to the plane and take a little break?" Robert said to Suri, putting an arm on her shoulder.

"Okay," she said, and turned to Gerald. "It was nice to meet you, Mr. Jan," Suri said, before heading back toward the plane.

Meanwhile, Gerald had politely declined Robert's request to come work alongside Robert and the rest of his team. They moved on to discussing Vishnu and how soon Gerald could launch.

"It's really impressive," Robert began. "So it'll be manned and orbit the comet, but what happens if the comet hits Earth? Will the astronaut be able to survive?"

Gerald stared coldly and intently at Robert before answering.

"The astronauts we take into space will most likely not come back," Gerald said. "The ship will have an escape pod capable of sending the astronaut back to Earth, but if there is no Earth to return to, it might not make a difference."

They were walking toward Jan's office now, and Robert noticed that Gerald shifted a bit uncomfortably when he answered this question. Robert stepped into Gerald's huge office.

It was encased by glass, but when Robert shut the door behind them, the glass turned opaque and looked crystallized. There were two big computers sitting atop an unassuming glass desk. Walls opposite the door were also glass, although not opaque. Robert looked out to the desert beyond Jan's office. He could see the heat trails just above the ground in the distance, and remembered the Los Angeles heat fondly from his time at UCLA. It was a more comfortable heat than the Houston humidity.

"I assumed that the astronauts wouldn't come back," Robert began. "Have you found volunteers willing to sacrifice their lives for this cause?"

"The astronauts we select will fully understand the likelihood of their return, but they will be saving the world with their sacrifice. We have several astronauts already considering this position. In fact, originally I wanted to do it, but I think I can better serve humanity by continuing to run things from down here. Also, as I am approaching fifty and do not have the proper training or high health standards to live in space, I have decided we must pick someone else."

"I agree," Robert said, jotting some things down in his notebook. "And now that I think of it, it might be better for you to run things from here. This ship will be a great help in the fight against the comet."

"Will we have open communication between us?" Gerald asked.

"Of course. And I can send you the information on some of the NASA astronauts who would make exemplary pilots for Vishnu."

Gerald thanked Robert. Robert realized that in order for Gerald's machine to work, he would need to convince the United States to give a private company access to its nuclear weapons, which would be difficult. Or maybe NASA could purchase the ship, and then affix the nuclear bombs to it.

"Mr. Jan?"

"Please, call me Gerald."

"You are aware that we might not even get to use

this machine, right? That trying to get this ship to leave Earth's orbit and then orbit Shiva is going to be extremely difficult? Almost impossible."

"Yes, doctor, I know. Before the comet, my goal in life was to get a colony of humans living on Mars before I died, but now I see a new goal: stop this comet from destroying the planet. And I think that having a ship orbit the comet is one of the best possible weapons we'll be able to use against it. We have to try."

"We'll see. If it works, I certainly agree with you. And thank God you're calling it a comet. The media keeps calling it a meteor," Robert replied, putting a hand on Gerald's shoulder.

"Well, comets are icy bodies from the—" Gerald began, musing on the differences between the two words.

Robert laughed, thinking that Gerald and he were going to work well together. He excused himself from Gerald's office and walked back to the airplane. After a brief safety intro, they took off for Los Alamos. It turns out they complete pre-flight safety intros on military jets, too.

3

WHEN EVERYTHING GOES RIGHT

Saturday, July 21, 2016
Near Clarendon, Texas

With only an hour or so left before the Sun set, the group still needed a place to sleep. Jeremy noticed that the amount of traffic on the road was very light, and there were no police patrols going on—none Jeremy could see anyway. He did notice a lot of military vehicles driving about. Many had pulled over citizens and were looking through their cars.

A few military vehicles tailgated them, but when they got close enough for Jeremy to see their faces out of the back of the window, they backed off. Whether they were trying to see who was in the car or it was simply a coincidence that they continued tailgating,

Jeremy couldn't be sure. Maybe it was the fact that they were kids. For whatever reason, they escaped the authorities' scrutiny. Jeremy noticed another Acura— the same model as Dustin's—had been pulled over.

"What do you think they got pulled over for?" Dustin asked.

It was hard to make out the faces in the car, since the darkness obscured them. Dustin watched the car disappear as some teenagers stepped out. Dustin could see only their teeth in the dim light.

"We should find a place to rest," Anna said, yawning.

Amazingly, she had driven the entire way. After another thirty minutes of driving, she saw a sign that read, *AMARILLO, 5 MILES*. Dustin was asleep on Jeremy's shoulder, and Karina stared off blankly toward the never-ending straight road. They were playing music from Anna's phone, which had shifted over to Taylor Swift. Jeremy actually liked it, but would never admit it to anyone. Suddenly Jeremy felt a familiar buzz in his pocket.

"I just got a text from my phone company," Jeremy said, careful to keep his voice down, "but it doesn't say anything. And the time stamp said it was sent two hours ago."

"Do you have service?" Anna asked.

"Yeah, but nothing is loading. I can't get any of the apps to work. Maybe the service's bandwidth is being used by the government to surveil us? Or Dr. Miller's team is using it somehow?"

Either way, we might have to go back to using regular maps soon, Jeremy thought. *Good thing I brought them.*

Jeremy looked outside at the speeding landscape, which was very flat, and watched the setting Sun fill the sky with a dazzling array of warm oranges, reds, and purples. They had seen a few hotels and motels along the way but unfortunately the lit "No Vacancy" signs shone through the dusk. They also saw there were no cars in their parking lots—another sign that travelers weren't welcome.

"Maybe we should just camp on the side of the

road," Anna mused, seeing a rest stop exit. Dustin snored in the backseat.

Suddenly Karina spoke up. "We should go to a church!"

"A church?" Jeremy said curiously.

"They would take us," Karina replied.

"Karina has a point," Jeremy replied, half joking. "They won't want to do anything immoral like refuse stranded travelers so close to Judgment Day."

Karina shot Jeremy a grimace, annoyed by his flippant response, but it was decided. They agreed to stop by a church. Anna drove on a little longer until Jeremy spotted a big white cross beside the freeway. She slowly pulled off, using her turn signal. Jeremy noticed that Karina had taken the cross she wore from deep down inside her shirt so that it displayed conspicuously on her chest.

The church parking lot was huge, but there were almost no cars. It was eerie driving up to the church, and Jeremy slowly woke up Dustin. When Dustin did finally wake up, he looked at the tall white cross towering over their car and groaned.

"Oh, God, not a church."

Dustin said he would clean up the car and watch it while the three others went to speak to the workers at the church.

"No," Jeremy said. "We have to go by the buddy system. Always have someone with you in Anarch-Merica."

"I'll stay with Dustin, then," Anna offered. "Karina, will you and Jeremy go see if there's anything there?"

"Yeah, sounds good."

Together, Jeremy and Karina walked toward the Amarillo Baptist church. Jeremy went to Europe with his family the summer of his freshman year, and he saw a lot of old Catholic and Protestant churches with beautiful stained glass and gargoyles and big statues of famous Christians. He thought they were so magnificent and showed a lot of history. Even though he had never been very religious, he loved the stories in the Bible, and being in those cathedrals had made him feel so small and humbled. The echoed footsteps of silent churchgoers always mesmerized him as he looked at the stained glass, trying to read the story in the pictures.

The Amarillo Baptist church, by contrast, was essentially a great big conference hall. The walls were white, and even though the ceiling was high, there weren't any ornate designs, organs, or stained glass windows, just rows and rows of fluorescent lights. The room was completely empty. Jeremy had noticed a car or two in the gargantuan parking lot, so he figured there had to be at least one person inside.

"Hello?" Jeremy said to the empty room.

His voice echoed back, giving the already creepy room a feeling like someone was watching them, but they were alone. Far away, past the rows of empty pews, the Crucifixion stood, staring at the ground. Jeremy looked away. It always made him somewhat uncomfortable, especially since he wasn't raised as a Christian. His father took him to church once when he was about eight because, "this is something that people do, Jer. They go here, and listen to stories together. Some of them are better people because of it, too, and some go for other reasons."

"Is that guy nailed to a cross?" Jeremy had asked his father innocently when they'd gone.

He'd said it too loud, though, and some people had heard him, glaring at both him and his father. It had made him perpetually uneasy around people who were very religious. He felt like people in church looked at him as if they were trying to read his mind. It was very unsettling.

"Anybody home?" he asked again.

Again, only his own echo answered him. Jeremy looked over at Karina, who was praying silently with her eyes closed. She opened them then and looked at him, then looked away.

"Karina, are you okay?" Jeremy asked gently.

"If this is it, then why am I so sad?" Karina choked, as if in mid-thought, and tried her hardest not to cry. "As a Christian we believe that this is supposed to be a good day. Judgment Day. This is when Jesus is supposed to come back and take us all into Heaven. Well, why am I so sad?"

Jeremy thought for a moment, putting his arm around his friend—the friend that had been a stranger only weeks ago. "Maybe because that means that a lot of people are going to die?"

That sounded a lot more comforting in my mind, Jeremy thought. He'd tried to say it as gently as possible too, but it didn't work. Karina started sobbing.

Darn it, he thought. *I wish I knew what to say to women.*

Jeremy and Karina walked by the rows of pews and down toward the podium where the pastor gave his sermons, stopping by doors to check if any were unlocked. No such luck. They checked behind the podium, but all the doors were sealed shut, and dejectedly they walked back to the front door of the Amarillo Baptist Church. They spotted Dustin and Anna in the backseat of the car, playing a game of cards.

"Gin!" Dustin yelled happily, so loudly that Jeremy could hear it even though the windows were closed.

Anna opened the car door when she saw they were close.

"Well?" she asked.

"No one was there," Jeremy said. "What should we do?"

They sat there together, eating some beans from a tin can—their second makeshift dinner—and discussed for the next hour whether they should open up their tents. Jeremy asserted they should find a place where three sides of their campsite would be blocked, and the other three thought he should stop being paranoid. Dustin argued they should camp inside the church.

Jeremy looked around. Night had almost supplanted dusk, and he swiped at some mosquitoes hovering by his ear. Then he saw a Subaru on the frontage road decelerate as it neared the church. The car turned into the parking lot, slowing so it wouldn't bottom out, and then continued at a slow pace directly toward their own car. Jeremy watched nervously as he fingered the pocketknife in his pocket, and Karina put down her can of beans.

An old man with a big straw hat waved at them through his open car window. They all braced, remembering what had happened to them at the gas station. Jeremy could also see an elderly woman sitting in the passenger seat. The man put the car in park. He stiffly got out and walked toward them with a pronounced limp.

"Howdy there, son," the man said once he got to Jeremy.

They all stood up and faced the man, who looked to be in his early sixties. The old woman in the passenger seat, with long blonde-but-greying hair, sat peering outside. Jeremy could see she was knitting.

When neither Jeremy nor his friends responded to the man, he continued. "Let me introduce myself. I'm Pastor Jack Westridge. I preside over this here church, and as I was driving home from the grocery, I noticed y'all in the lot."

Pastor Jack stopped talking then and waited, thinking that he would get some sort of response, which he did not get. When Jeremy and his friends said nothing, waiting for Pastor Jack to continue, the pastor looked down at his feet.

Jack was wearing a white collared shirt with a bolo tie, cowboy boots, dirty jeans, and a gun. Jeremy stared at the gun and Jack noticed.

"Ah, yes. Well, I'm going to go very slowly and move that, all right? That way we can have a more civil discourse. That does mean y'all might need to speak up though."

Jeremy tensed, and so did his friends, but Pastor Jack was true to his word. He slowly removed the gun and placed it on the ground. Then, to their surprise, he carefully kicked it toward them. It stopped, still slightly spinning on its handle, directly in between Jeremy and the Pastor.

"What's your name, son?" Jack asked.

"Jeremy Genser."

"Well, Jeremy, I know these are unusual times we

have caught ourselves in, but God has taught me to take in a stranger instead of treating him strangely. If you'd like, you and your friends are welcome to spend the night at my house. My wife, Noreen, is a fantastic cook."

Pastor Jack motioned back with his arm toward the elderly woman. Karina looked elated, and was already nodding her head, making Jack smile.

"Could you excuse us briefly, Pastor?" Jeremy asked.

"Certainly. I'll give you folks a minute."

They leaned in together as Jack stepped away, and began to whisper, while Jeremy kept an eye on the gun and its owner.

"We should do it; they are good Christians," Karina said, almost immediately.

"Remember we only trust each other . . . " Anna countered.

"Do you think we can trust them?" Dustin asked.

"I think we should go," Jeremy said, and the others looked at him in surprise.

"You think we should trust them?" Anna asked.

"I'm not sure yet," Jeremy began, "but I think he does want to help us. And plus, they both look like they're in their seventies, what could they do? He couldn't shoot us all."

They all looked up at Jack and his wife, who was continuing to knit obliviously in the passenger seat. Then they turned their heads back down.

"Vote?" Anna proffered.

They agreed by nodding their heads.

"Those in favor of going with Jack?" Anna proffered.

Anna, Karina, and Jeremy nodded, with Dustin saying nothing.

"I guess that means we go," Dustin said.

"Jack?" Jeremy called, "we would love to take you up on your offer."

"Excellent! Ah, that is excellent. Noreen dear! Did you hear that? These wonderful youngsters are going to stay with us tonight."

Noreen still made no motion proving she could

hear, but when she finally looked up from her knitting, she smiled warmly at the group.

Jeremy gulped nervously, hoping he wasn't making a mistake. Jack told them to follow him in his car. They got in and drove through the huge church parking lot, and there was an old house adjoining the far end of the church. The drive only took about two minutes.

Jeremy walked in and noticed a big difference between the church and Pastor Jack's house. While the church had no defining religious artwork—aside from the Crucifixion—the home was filled with religious artwork. Most noticeably, above a fireplace in the living room hung a haunting painting of the Virgin Mary.

"Y'all are welcome to sleep on the couch, and there is a small bedroom over here if you want to take a look. Perhaps you two girls can take the room, and the boys can have the couches?"

The small bedroom was painted bright green.

Stuffed animals were piled on each of the twin beds, which took up most of the room.

"Of course!" Anna responded. "This is amazing, thank you so much."

"Great," Pastor Jack exclaimed. "Well, if you want to get freshened up before dinner there is a bathroom over there."

After a quick trip to the bathroom for the four of them, they all sat down to dinner, which Jeremy looked at disdainfully. It looked better than the cold black beans they ate, but barely. Noreen, Pastor Jack's wife, roughly plopped down a big bowl of murky liquid filled with meat, potatoes, soggy carrots, and peas. Despite this the group munched it down eagerly.

"Thank you, Noreen!" Anna gurgled in between mouthfuls.

"No problem, my pleasure, sweetheart," Noreen replied, before asking, "So, where y'all headed?"

"Up to Colorado," Jeremy answered. "We are visiting some family."

"Oh, y'all are siblings then?"

"Um, cousins," Karina cut in. "We are cousins."

They continued to eat in relative silence, until suddenly the phone rang. It wasn't a cell phone ring, and it startled Jeremy, who hadn't heard a landline phone since he was around four years old. It was a pervasive ringing, loud and obnoxious, and there was no ignore button or "reply with text" option to stop the ring. A landline telephone ringing was a social event; everyone's heads whirled in the direction of the phone.

"I wonder who could be calling during dinner . . . " Pastor Jack mused, getting up slowly. Everyone stopped eating while he answered the phone on the second ring. "Hello? Ah, hi honey. How are you? Say, we are in the middle of—" Then Pastor Jack's expression darkened. "What? What? Are you serious? Oh my God . . . channel two?"

"Honey?" Noreen said.

Pastor Jack gave his wife a look which Jeremy could not decipher, and walked to the adjoining living room to turn on the television. He was still holding onto the phone, speaking.

"I'm just happy you are okay . . . I love you too."

When Jeremy peered around Pastor Jack and toward the TV, his heart sank, like it does when you're on a roller coaster and the click-click of the gears forces you high away from the Earth, and there's only one way out—straight down.

One of the IMPs—the nuclear missiles he had been hearing about—had had a faulty first-stage engine. As it tried to make its ascent to Shiva, it began to fall back to Earth. Jeremy could hear a CNN reporter saying something about the primary engine. *How could this have happened?* Jeremy thought.

Instead of falling harmlessly into the Atlantic Ocean—which was meant to occur—the nuclear weapon was making its way toward the city of Miami. Jeremy knew that rockets were purposefully sent into the atmosphere in such a way that if something happens, they fall harmlessly into the ocean. They could view the Miami skyline from a news helicopter. The falling nuke was just a small blip in the sky, but it was descending fast.

Jeremy watched the CNN video of the nuclear weapon slowly losing altitude. He was vaguely aware of Pastor Jack turning up the volume on the TV.

" . . . Residents of South Florida and Miami have begun evacuating, but as you can see, the highways are all bumper to bumper. People are getting out of their cars and running now . . . "

There were large gaps in the reporter's speech, and Karina looked away from the TV as the bomb inched down the screen. Then, as they watched the nuclear weapon fall slowly down to Earth, two separate missiles came from the north and sped toward the falling nuke. The first one approached the nuke. Then there was a collision—missile on missile—and then the entire screen went white.

Everyone watching the screen gasped, and then Noreen began to cry.

"Dear Lord . . . " Pastor Jack murmured sadly.

Jeremy could say nothing as the connection to the news helicopter cut out, and CNN switched to their newsroom where four stunned reporters sat, unsure of what to tell the public. Finally one spoke.

"A nuclear bomb has just exploded a quarter of a mile above Miami, Florida."

4

A GIFT

July 22, 2016
Outside Amarillo, Texas

Jeremy woke up groggily on the couch. It was a very deep and comfortable couch, and even though he'd had a full night's sleep he felt like he'd only slept an hour or two. His eyes were puffy. He looked over at the TV, which was still on. A reporter explained that Martial Law had been declared in the non-revolting areas of the United States. Then Jeremy fell back asleep.

When he woke up again, a reporter spoke about the disaster in Miami. The death count from the IMP impact was still unknown. *So many people*, Jeremy thought. It was difficult for him—for anyone—to imagine. Jeremy looked around and saw Dustin snoring in the small loveseat.

"Evacuation of around ten thousand citizens was successful," the reporter said, "through NASA's early warning system. The military also fired two missiles which successfully intercepted the nuclear device and detonated it in the air. This greatly lessened the nuclear fallout from the explosion, and saved an untold number of lives. Still, we are projecting that the nuclear explosion has taken the lives of tens of thousands. Preliminary reports are estimating the casualties in the hundreds of thousands.

"I'm here with Arnold Jackson, one of the evacuees in the Miami disaster, who thankfully made it out alive. Arnold, can you tell us what happened?"

A quavering voice sounded over the incoming video feed of a decimated Miami. "It was horrible, just horrible. I was just driving home from work, listening to the radio. I heard the evacuation message and I drove straight north. I saw a missile hit something just above Miami, and then everything lit up. I had to look away—it was brighter than the Sun. It's just horrible. I saw people who were outside when the bomb hit, and it looked like their skin was falling off. When I looked up I saw the mushroom cloud starting to grow above Miami. It's just horrible, and it was a mistake by our own government? What does NASA have to say for themselves? How could our government allow this to happen? I can't believe it, it was just awful."

The reporter spoke again, replying to the man, "It certainly is awful, and there are a lot of questions that need to be answered about this terrible event. For those of you just joining us, the United States has accepted responsibility for the Miami disaster."

Jeremy turned off the television, and walked into the kitchen. Noreen was wearing a frock that looked like it was from the 1950s. She had puffy eyes, too.

"Care for some coffee, honey?"

Jeremy nodded and sipped at the burning liquid without cream or sugar. It was bitter.

"The TV said there is to be a curfew now," Noreen said.

Jeremy tried to respond but the coffee had burned his tongue and the top of his mouth.

"Do you think you'll still go to Denver?" Noreen asked.

"Yes," Jeremy managed, thinking it was more important than ever to get to Vail as soon as possible.

"I wanted to give you something, but don't tell my husband, please."

Noreen pulled a metallic object from a fold of her long frock. It was a gun—a nine millimeter caliber Smith & Wesson handgun. Out of a small pocket in her dress she pulled a small grey box, which held around one hundred extra rounds of ammunition.

Jeremy stood in shock as the little old lady held the weapon, thrusting it into his hands.

"I don't know if this is such a good idea," Jeremy began. "I don't really want this."

"Trust me, honey. This is the end of the world we are talking about here. You need to be careful."

"With a gun?"

"Especially with one."

She quickly showed Jeremy the safety, the ammunition release, and the trigger. Since Jeremy was left-handed the ammunition release required him to wrap his pointer-trigger finger all the way around the handle of the gun. Noreen taught him quickly how to use the sights.

"So, you line the middle bump all the way down the barrel with the two next to the barrel. Make sure the middle bump fits exactly in between the other two. It should make a nice little line of three bumps . . . "

As she spoke, the old grandmother-looking Noreen shut her eye and aimed the gun around the room, finally settling on Jeremy. His heart unconsciously skipped a beat—it was the second time someone had aimed a gun at him in one week. It was a mystifying sensation to stare down the barrel of a gun. Then she lowered the gun and handed the hilt to Jeremy.

"Now you try."

Gingerly he held the weapon—guns always seemed heavier to him than he first thought—and took it up. He closed one eye and took aim at the kitchen cabinets.

"Remember, it's a big responsibility to hold that thing. With it, you can choose who lives and who dies. It's important to know that you should never play God. Only use it as a very last resort."

"Thank you, Noreen," Jeremy replied. "I'll be careful."

Jeremy put the gun in the waistband of his pants, pulling his shirt over it just like he always saw in the movies. His pants sagged a little bit until he tightened his belt so the gun wouldn't fall out.

By this time the others had woken up, their eyes also red and puffy from crying, and got ready to leave. Together they said goodbye to Pastor Jack and Noreen. Noreen gave Jeremy a knowing nod as they wished each other good luck.

"Are y'all sure you don't want to stay here?" Pastor Jack asked. "You know all of God's children are welcome here."

"That's very kind of you," Anna began, "but we

must make our way up to Denver. Thank you for everything."

"Well, all right, then, but be careful. And remember that just because it looks like the world is about to end, we must still remain good, and follow the path to righteousness. Treat people the way you would want to be treated, or better. And good luck. It's a dangerous world out there, now more than ever."

Jack and Noreen waved from their porch as the group got into the car and started their long drive north.

· · ·

Robert walked toward the cafeteria to refill his cup of coffee. His eyes were bloodshot from lack of sleep. He'd been awake all night working with the rest of NASA and the military on the disaster in Miami. The events of the past day were devastating. It was unclear if Robert's team would even continue to work as the lead in the project to avert the comet.

One wall of the cafeteria windows pointed west toward the New Mexican scenery. He saw Suri drinking her coffee, staring at the New Mexico hills surrounding Los Alamos. They were truly breathtaking.

J. Robert Oppenheimer, the man who led the Manhattan Project and created the world's first atomic bomb, had chosen this area to lead the project partly because of its beauty. He thought it would be calming for the scientists. Now, instead of creating an atomic bomb that would destroy people, they were trying to figure out ways to build new and better ones that would save people by destroying a comet.

Robert had been pleased with their progress with Shiva. In the past two months they had launched fourteen rockets out of Earth's orbit and toward Shiva. Four of them malfunctioned on their way, and communication was lost. Nine of them were on course as planned, with two of those acting as observational satellites. The last one, however, was the source of

Robert's despair. It was the rocket that tumbled back to Earth, destroying an entire city.

"Hi, Robert, I found it," Suri said, as Robert walked up to Suri's table.

Though she was in the cafeteria, she had her computer and was hard at work going over the engine's computer code. It was hard for her to think of anything else besides, *Miami is gone.* It was hard to believe, and the effect that it had on the population in just one day was terrifying. President Chaplin enacted Martial Law. Gangs overthrew major metropolises. Los Angeles and Chicago fell to the gangs, joining San Francisco and Seattle as places which no longer referred to themselves as part of the United States of America. Suri couldn't believe how fast it seemed anarchy was setting in. Despite all of this, Suri worked diligently on figuring out the exact reason for the IMP's failure.

Thus far, they had linked the IMP's engine failure to a faulty O-ring in one of the rocket boosters, which incidentally had also been the cause of NASA's

Challenger disaster three decades earlier. Suri had begun searching the code they wrote for this particular booster for inconsistencies or some further mistake.

The search took only a few hours, because Suri found a patch in the code *forcing* the engine to malfunction and fall back to Earth. Suri showed the patch to Robert, who asked, "Who did we assign to do this code?"

Robert stared at the patch incredulously. *Could this be a sabotage by someone here?* he wondered.

"I did the code," Suri muttered. "This was me, but it wasn't. I didn't do this patch, I swear. Someone else went over it—see? Here's the time stamp, two days after I finished the rest of this code. And this IP address—it's not mine."

Robert read from Suri's computer, astonished.

"So someone else hacked into our servers and inserted this code, or someone at NASA did it."

"It looks like it, but who would do that?" Suri asked aghast.

"Let's talk to Brighton," Robert replied.

Suri closed her computer and together they hustled over to Secretary Brighton's office, who looked like he'd aged a year in only one night.

"It wasn't an O-ring failure," Robert began. "I won't go over it in too much detail, but this highlighted code here . . . " Robert showed the Secretary of State Suri's highlighted code. "This patch that goes on for around a hundred lines wasn't Dr. Lahdka's."

"So what does that mean?" Secretary Brighton asked, squinting at the screen.

"It means," Robert replied impatiently, "that either someone at NASA wanted to prevent this missile from entering the orbit, or someone else hacked our servers."

Secretary Brighton spoke very slowly. "And Miami? Are you suggesting that the destruction of Miami was a terrorist attack?"

Robert and Suri looked at each other.

"I don't know," Suri began. "The code they entered was programmed to flood the engine all at once, which put the O-rings past the normal pressures they were meant to handle. But I don't know how it drifted back toward land and hit Miami. I think that was just—" Suri paused, unable to finish her sentence.

"—really, really," Robert grimaced, "really bad luck."

Inside, however, Robert still felt like there was something missing about the incident.

Secretary Brighton closed his eyes, rubbing his temples. Then he got up and closed the door to his office, and turned around.

"Doctors, you are aware of the hacker by the name One Union Anarchist? The one that ultimately forced us to reveal the truth about the comet?"

Robert and Suri nodded.

"Okay, well, the peace and security of the United States is not as stable as we've been advertising it to be. The Union Anarchists and other terrorist groups have been active in many places around the United States. Los Alamos is now one of the most heavily guarded places in the world, aside from the White House."

Robert tried to contain his anger. "What do you

mean? Is it possible that we are compromised—that there is a traitor in our midst?"

"It's unlikely, but possible. I'm sorry, right now there's not much more I can say," Secretary Brighton answered. "Thank you for bringing this news to me. I will tell you more when I can."

Robert and Suri excused themselves from the Secretary, and went back to their joined office. *From now on, we'll have to double and triple-check everything,* Robert thought. *There might even be someone against us on the inside. Unbelievable . . .*

"That project to use the LSST, do you have any thoughts?" Robert asked, referring to the telescope they were using to take photos of the comet.

"Yes," Suri replied, but her mind was elsewhere. "It could be good to get it up and running. But if it still doesn't work that'd be a problem."

"Maybe."

Later in the day, Robert and Suri sat next to each other, both working on their computers, feeling numb. Neither of them had typed anything for a full minute.

"Want to go for a walk?" Robert asked.

Suri said yes, and they took the car to a nearby trail. Robert saw footsteps on the ground. He imagined they were J. Robert Oppenheimer's. They walked in silence for a while, feeling the hot New Mexico sunlight against their bodies. As they walked along, both of them had Miami on their minds. Both of them wanted to say something and nothing at the same time, and ask each other what they were thinking about. When they turned a corner in the trail, they saw a small deer, who froze upon noticing a human intrusion on the land.

As the deer—a mature, strong doe—stared back at Robert and Suri, they froze as well, and for a moment both of them forgot about the largest nuclear disaster ever on American soil. Then, as fast as it froze, the deer leapt away, back into the forest of trees and undergrowth. Suri and Robert looked at each other, and realized the deer's presence made them each forget about Miami for a few seconds. Then they both burst into tears.

• • •

As Jeremy drove north along the freeway, he saw the great Rocky Mountains looming in the west, while to the east lay the great plains of eastern Colorado, Kansas, and Missouri, which stretched all the way to the Mississippi River. Everyone's minds were fixated on Miami, but no one managed to say anything. The casualties were reported to be in the hundreds of thousands, but the military's use of the anti-ballistic missiles had drastically reduced the death toll. Even so, people in the area were notified to evacuate and there hadn't been enough time. The freeways were bumper to bumper, so people got out of their cars and began to run. It was hard for the group driving along Interstate 25 not to think about it, but they had problems of their own to deal with, too.

At twenty-five miles to Denver, things began to

change. The first thing they noticed were the road signs, which were entirely spray painted in black. Jeremy also noticed that the interstate signs, posted every few miles to remind drivers what road they were on, were blacked out as well. Then, as they passed under one of the signs for Grand Junction, they saw the symbol for Anarchy—the letter "A" with a circle around it across the entire sign.

There was a normal amount of traffic for a major American city. If it wasn't for the increase in the anarchist graffiti, they wouldn't have noticed anything different about Denver.

The rest of the signs were even less helpful. Whoever had been spray painting the signs must have gotten a little overexcited, because the closer they got to Denver, the higher the frequency of the black signs. By the time they got within five miles, every sign was an ominous black rectangle. It was so obvious that eventually Jeremy had to ask the question, "Guys? Are we sure we should go through Denver? These blacked out signs are kind of creepy. Maybe we should avoid the city."

Having grown up in the world of cell phones, everyone reached into their pockets to grab the little metallic computers to check other routes to Vail. They were all dismayed to find that they were not functioning.

"What should we do?" Dustin asked.

Jeremy thought for a moment before taking the road that looked like it headed toward the mountains.

"Let's go this way. Also, Dustin, I stuck a road map in the glove compartment. Try to find out where we are. Vail is in the Rockies, so for now, let's go toward them."

"Nice," Dustin agreed.

They took an exit that headed in the right direction, but before long they had to stop for gas.

"I guess we can make sure we are on the right path," Anna remarked.

"I know where we are going," Dustin said, looking at the road map.

The gas and lodging signs pointing toward the off-ramp were not blacked out like the interstate's and the larger signs near Denver. As the road veered off to the right, Jeremy became aware of an obstruction in the road—a row of overturned shopping carts. Jeremy slowed and drove around it.

"Did you guys see that?" he asked.

"Weird," Karina agreed.

Jeremy drove under the freeway and went two blocks until he saw the gas station. The town looked a lot different than Dallas, with boarded-up windows and anarchy flags everywhere.

"Maybe Denver knew about the comet before everyone else?" Dustin mused. "Otherwise, how could it look like this so fast?"

Jeremy didn't reply, but did agree with him. He continued to drive until he stopped at a light. Then he turned right to enter the gas station, and slammed on the breaks, just in time to avoid a collision.

Standing in front of the car was an incredibly disheveled homeless man. He looked drunk, leaning left and right, and was sweating profusely. He wore several overcoats, even though the temperature was balmy.

"What the heck," Dustin yelped. "Can you just drive around him?"

"He's pretty close. Here, I'll back up."

Jeremy looked down at the stick shift and flung it into reverse, but as he looked back through the rear window, he shuddered. A second figure blocked their escape route, and for the third time that week, he found himself looking down the barrel of a gun.

This time it was much larger than the small barrel that Noreen had given him. This time it was a shotgun. *So now it's two barrels actually*, Jeremy thought randomly. Jeremy raised his hands from the steering wheel and looked at the owner of the gun. Whoever it was wore a mask.

When he looked forward again the apparently homeless gentlemen had pulled a shotgun from inside one of his many overcoats. The robber in front of the car tilted the barrel to the side. Then the man behind the car walked over to Jeremy's window, and motioned for Jeremy to lower the window. Dustin cursed.

"What do we do? What do we do?" he whispered frantically.

"I don't think there's anything we can do."

Jeremy slowly moved his left hand over to roll the window down. It seemed like such an insignificant thing to do, but the last barrier between him and that gun was gone. The man reached in with his hand and grabbed the keys to the car. Then he unlocked the door.

"License and registration, please," the mask said.

"What?" Jeremy asked, confused.

On the other side of the car, the homeless drunkard, who seemed completely sober at this point, had opened Karina's car door.

"Stop it," the homeless-looking robber said to the masked one. "He's just messin' with you. Get out of the car before we blast you! Now!"

Jeremy looked back and forth between the two.

He guessed the masked person was female judging by the voice.

When Jeremy played basketball, he could always tell the caliber of player by the way they held the ball in their hand. It was a comfort thing. The best players held the ball like it was just another part of their body. This is what the shotgun looked like in this woman's hand—like it was just another part of her body. Jeremy gulped.

"Let's just do what they say . . . " Anna coaxed.

"Listen to the pretty one, bud," the masked woman said.

Slowly they exited the car, making sure to make their hands steady and visible at all times. They got out of the car and stood in a row with the two thugs opposite them.

"The earrings," the woman said slowly.

Anna took hers off and placed them in the man's free hand.

"Yours too, sweetie," she said to Karina.

"But . . . "

"Jesus, Karina, just give it to them," Jeremy breathed.

Slowly, the masked woman walked behind the foursome. Jeremy could feel her walking back toward the trailer still hitched to the Acura. He could hear the couple whispering about something. Then he heard more footsteps. Suddenly, there was a loud "Bang!"

Anna and Karina screamed, Jeremy whirled around, wincing in anticipation of an incoming shotgun blast. Dustin closed his eyes.

There was a sharp metallic bang, and Jeremy saw that the masked woman had not shot them, but opted to shoot the trailer hitch of the U-Haul instead. There were a few more blasts of the shotgun, followed by an argument between the two robbers, where both of them shouted at each other. Apparently, shooting the trailer hitch hadn't released it. Jeremy looked on, thinking that it would be amusing if they weren't getting robbed. Then the masked woman unhitched the U-Haul with her hands.

Jeremy watched in despair as the couple hopped

into his car and drove off, leaving them stranded in the middle of the road.

"I can't believe it . . . " Jeremy muttered to himself. "Gas stations suck."

"Well, at least they didn't take the U-haul . . . " Dustin conceded.

He's always seeing the glass half full, Jeremy thought.

"But they did take the key to it. It was attached to the key to the Acura," Karina reminded the group.

Jeremy slowly walked over to the U-Haul and the preposterously large padlock he had purchased. On the plus side, Jeremy's overly careful packing list paid off because inside the U-Haul, they had four fully loaded backpacking backpacks and enough water to last them several days. Unfortunately, water is extremely heavy, and you need a lot of it to live. Luckily he'd put the backpacks in the U-Haul instead of in the trunk, which had been Dustin's idea. Jeremy stared at the bolted padlock while Dustin searched around for a rock to smash it with. Slowly, Jeremy pulled up his shirt to reveal the gun he had.

"Woah," Anna exclaimed.

"Where did you get that?" Karina asked.

Jeremy shared the story of his conversation with Noreen and the gift he received shortly after. The gun felt heavy.

It was a strange yet relieving feeling that the first thing he had to shoot was his own U-Haul. He touched the barrel of the gun to the curved metal of the lock. He took a deep breath, closed his eyes, and fired.

When he opened them he saw all three of his friends covering their ears. Then he looked down at the padlock, which was relatively unharmed. He'd missed.

"Maybe just go for the whole lock?" Dustin offered.

Jeremy nodded, and took a step back. He aimed the weapon at the padlock, and fired three times. He'd fired so quickly that the lock shook a few times back and forth. Jeremy inspected the lock, and was surprised at what little damage had been done to it.

"Hmm," Jeremy said, "that didn't work. Also, we

might not want to do that again. The bullet could ricochet and hit one of us."

Jeremy could think of only one way to open the lock, and it would take a while. He found a few large rocks in a little park across from the gas station, and began smashing the rocks against the padlock and the latches of the U-Haul door. After ten minutes, Dustin took a turn to hack away at the lock.

Then Karina, and then Anna, and then Jeremy again. This continued for a whole hour until finally the latch broke off the U-Haul. The lock was still shut tight, but with the latch broken, Jeremy opened the door and looked inside. He grabbed the backpacks and then noticed all their other materials he'd managed to stuff into the U-Haul. The tools, drills, the generator, suitcases full of food and canisters of gas, and water, and much more. All the things they would have to leave behind.

"We could just try to steal a car . . . " Dustin offered.

"Or find one. There's got to be people that aren't

using theirs, just settling in for Judgment Day, you know."

Jeremy eyed the barbeque, which he had thrown in simply because they had the space. The barbeque was an easy thing to leave.

Finally, the group voted on what to do with the stuff, and decided that full backpacks were enough to carry. Jeremy and Dustin pulled the U-Haul off the road, and tried their best to hide it amongst the trees across from the gas station. They decided stealing a car would be too dangerous. The trailer was still very conspicuous, but figured that if there was a chance they would return, it would be nice to have some supplies waiting for them. He also hid some food under the U-Haul and in other areas in the park, just in case they needed to go back there one day.

"So, what now?" Anna asked. "We walk?"

"Now, we walk . . . " Jeremy answered, grabbing Anna's hand.

5

SOUTHGLENN

July 23, 2016
Southglenn, Colorado

Jeremy and the gang walked somewhat aimlessly down the street toward the looming Rocky Mountains. They figured that since they had two tents, eventually they'd get out of the city and be able to set up a camp. Jeremy pretended it would be like a vacation. Their phones were unreliable in Denver, but Anna managed to send a "we're safe" text to her parents. Jeremy said the same thing to his parents when they were on the road.

Jeremy felt like prey without the Acura. They walked along, four teens wearing big backpacks, almost asking for someone to take their things. They were silent for a while, and Jeremy grabbed the radio he had stuffed in his backpack to see if there were any government signals or announcements. Jeremy had put a radio in each of their bags so they could communicate with each other if they got separated in Vail.

Jeremy also thought that radio could become the method of communication for the government if their hold over the people collapsed, since satellites might be tied up in tracking the comet. Jeremy turned the radio on, tuning to different stations and trying to find National Public Radio. Luckily, just when Jeremy found the station, a voice was speaking. It was President Chaplin!

" . . . and a code-red curfew is now in effect. Anyone out past sunset may be arrested by either the police or the military. The comet J312 is two years away from a possible collision. Anyone who is willing to work in the effort against the comet please call the government hotline 7-1-1. There is work to be done, and you will be paid for your commitment. I repeat, please call 7-1-1. For the separatist states of San

Francisco, Seattle, and Denver, I would urge its citizens to call as well, and move to help. We must work together to defeat the mightiest foe in our nation's—our world's—history.

"Our nation has already suffered a great tragedy—Miami. The world's top scientists are working around the clock to try to save the planet. They need more time in order to make sure there are no more mistakes. We have no more time, but we have more manpower. People like you. People with knowledge and a desire to help. If you are up for the challenge, please call our hotline. I repeat, we need you."

Jeremy stopped listening to the radio as his mind turned to Denver. *So,* he thought, *we are officially not in the United States of America.* It actually made sense since, in addition to the road signs covered in graffiti, he hadn't seen a single military van or police car since they'd reached the Denver suburbs.

It was getting dark quickly. The most difficult thing about their new life was the uncertainty about the future. Jeremy tried not to think about their lack of stability, but it felt like a fly at his ear, buzzing all the time. Even when he'd forget about it, soon enough the fly would return, and he would remember that the government was crumbling, and the world was about to end.

"Hey, look!" Dustin exclaimed, pointing forward.

Jeremy shook himself out of his reverie, and when he looked up he saw an open city park just ahead. The park was large, maybe three square blocks, and a fair amount of it was occupied by tents, creating a kind of tent-village. People milled about inside, and there were cooking fires with smoke climbing to the sky.

"You guys think we should set up camp? I think I have the gas stove in my bag. We could make some rice and beans?" Karina offered.

"Maybe we should camp alone instead of with these people?" Anna asked.

They all thought for a moment, until Jeremy replied, "I think it might be better to kind of meld in with the herd. If looters come, it would be easy to pick us off if we set up alone, you know?"

The group nodded collectively and walked into the park and toward a wooded area for a bit of cover. Inside the trees, Jeremy saw the expanse of the tent city. It was much larger than he originally thought. Furthermore, the tents were all new—like they were just bought from REI. The same could be said of the barbeques the campers were using. The group walked up to the edge of the encampment and picked a spot to stay the night.

Dustin and Jeremy worked on setting up the tents in the dusk while Karina and Anna cooked. People were looking at them. *We are probably twenty years younger than every person here*, Jeremy thought.

With the two tents erected, Dustin leaned against the trunk of the tree. Then he felt lazy watching the girls cook food for everyone, and decided to go look around for some firewood. As he walked around he thought about calling the 7-1-1 number that President Chaplin had mentioned. He replayed in his mind the part where Chaplin had said, "If you want to help . . ."

"Oh!" Dustin exclaimed.

Lost in his own world, Dustin had neglected to watch where he was going, and had tripped over a woman crouching on the ground. The woman had been looking for firewood as well, and both of them fell to the ground in a heap. The firewood she had collected was pinned under both of them, and Dustin awkwardly apologized for essentially body-slamming her.

"I'm so sorry!"

"Oh, that's alright, don't worry," the woman replied, looking over and smiling at Dustin.

The woman looked to be in her late twenties, and wore very expensive clothes for being in a homeless encampment. She had on an expensive-looking necklace. Twigs stuck to her white blouse.

"I'm Dustin," Dustin said, brushing the twigs stuck to his own shirt.

"Nice to meet you, Dustin. My name is Janice. Janice Effran."

They shook hands. Dustin thought her last name

sounded familiar, but paid it no mind, asking if she was living in the park for a long time.

"I've been here about two weeks . . . What about you?"

Dustin got the feeling she wanted to tell him more, but let it go.

"I actually just arrived from Houston with a few friends. We just made dinner. Do you want to join us?"

It looked like Janice was slightly taken aback by his offer, but composed herself quickly and agreed. Together they walked back to their camp with two armfuls of firewood. It was dark by the time they returned, and the group was huddled around the small cooking stove where the beans were warming up.

Dustin introduced Janice to the group and began making the fire.

They ate in silence. Having someone eat with them was a lot more awkward than Dustin had anticipated. With the fire going, though, they all fell into the trance of watching the flames dance. Jeremy gave

Dustin a look, which said: *I thought we were supposed to keep to ourselves?* Jeremy looked up every once in a while at the other encampments. In some, people were singing and dancing and yelling.

"They're all on drugs," Janice muttered, noticing Jeremy looking around.

"What? Really?" Karina chimed.

"They used to all be white-collar workers, you know, just working the nine-to-five every day, and once they learned about the meteor, they decided to leave it all behind and party until the world ends."

"Wow."

More silence and flickering flames.

"So," Janice began, "have you run into any trouble? I've heard there have been a lot of car accidents lately."

Jeremy looked briefly at the others to ask if he should be honest or not, but they didn't help. "A few, actually. We got our car stolen today."

"What? That's awful! How did that happen?"

"It was actually just a few miles from here."

Janice sighed. "I can believe it. Things haven't been

particularly good here the past few months. Denver has known about the comet for a while now."

"How?" Jeremy asked, intrigued.

"I'm not exactly sure, but I do know that the hippy and conspiracy theorist culture has something to do with it. People have always thought something crazy was going to happen, so when it did, they looked at the dots and found them relatively easy to connect. Chile, Project Mars, the increase in military presence, all of it. When Anonymous released the data about the meteor, everyone just believed it."

"And the military?"

"We pushed them back up to Fort Collins pretty quickly . . . "

Jeremy got the feeling Janice wanted to say more, but he didn't push her.

Janice ate her beans slowly, one at a time. By the time the rest of them were done with dinner she had barely eaten half of her bowl.

"There were other signs about it, too," Janice began.

"Signs about what?"

"The coming end of the world."

They stared at the fire awhile. Jeremy glanced through the dark haze at the other campers, who were getting raucous. *At least no one will come to harm us tonight; they're probably all too drugged up*, he thought. But he couldn't be sure—these white-collar workers had given up hope in life and turned to drugs. Jeremy made a mental note to assign a rotating watch for the night.

"What other signs did you see?" Jeremy asked.

Again, Janice hesitated, but then she spoke, asking a simple question. "Do you know who I am?" she asked.

When none of them replied, she continued, "Well, I guess I'm not really somebody, but my father, Elliot Effran, owns Dish Network."

She waited for a response. "So?" Jeremy asked. "That means he's kind of rich or something, right?"

"Forbes says online that he has seventeen billion dollars, but it's more like thirty. My father is one cutthroat businessman. And if the world is going to end, you better believe he's going to be one of the first to know. So, he told me."

"When did he know?" Jeremy asked, curious to see if he knew before he and Anna found Dr. Miller and confronted him in that dingy bar.

"One of his former business contacts in Russia spoke to him about it. My father is heavily connected, and since he works a lot with satellites, the Russians spoke to him shortly after they found out."

"Oh! They found out before we did then, Jer," Anna said.

Janice looked confused so they filled her in on their little adventure. She listened intently to Jeremy, while the fire lighted her face.

"Wow! What a story!" she remarked. "You guys are pretty gutsy."

Jeremy looked over at Anna, and they smiled at each other.

Janice continued. "After my father got the call from his connections in Russia, he called a few of his friends. These are all people who are at least as rich as my father, like several of his Russian oligarch friends, and the old money types, like oil billionaire heirs. A group of them all got together right when they found out and discussed what to do. When they realized that the world was going to end in . . . two years from now . . . they figured that they should get off of it."

Janice paused to catch her breath, and Jeremy spoke up. "Get off it? What do you mean—leave for Mars or something? They don't believe that NASA can stop the comet?"

Janice shook her head, dismayed. "They don't. And the Miami disaster proved it. A lot of uncertainty is going on in the world right now, and even the scientists don't know exactly what's going to happen. I mean, they have their calculations and their assumptions, and even though they definitely know more than us, even they aren't sure. The government couldn't even stop three major cities from revolting; maybe they aren't as strong as we think. The meteor is going to hit us if we don't do anything to stop it. The rockets being sent up to hit it *might* change its course. Or they might do nothing."

"Comet," Anna said, "It's a comet."

"Oh, okay. Anyway, deep in the Rocky Mountains, north of Vail in a deep valley, the world's elite are building an ark. It's basically a really big spaceship. It's not like those big ships in *Star Wars*, but it'll be the biggest thing to leave Earth. I know this because I was helping with it, and I've watched it get bigger for the past five months. The wealthiest people in the world made billions of dollars exploiting the Earth—its natural resources and its people—and now that it's going to be blown up by a big *comet*, they're leaving it."

Jeremy sat in silence for a minute and looked at the fire. Then Dustin spoke up. "Are you going with them?" he asked Janice.

"I was . . . but I don't know. They are going to orbit the Earth for as long as they can. They'll take readings of the Earth before, during, and after impact. Then, when they figure it's safe to return, they will."

"Wow," Karina muttered.

"So that's their plan," Janice said, "and I decided that it wasn't for me. I wanted to at least see what the rest of the world was doing in the face of disaster. So far I'm not too impressed." Janice looked over at the revelers in the campsites next to them. One of the larger guys, a rotund, balding man with glasses, stumbled around his campsite, almost knocking over the barbeque.

"God has a plan for us," Karina said confidently.

Janice didn't hear Karina, and asked, "And what is your plan?"

"Well," Jeremy began, "we are on our way to Vail, where my girlfriend Anna's family has a cabin. We figure it'll be safe to live there. I don't want to be in the big city if something bad happens. Our parents are still down in Houston, and our cell phones have stopped working. We were supposed to drive up there today, but now that our car got stolen, we don't really know what we should do."

Janice was silent for a moment before answering. "I could give you a ride if you really need one."

Jeremy and the group looked at each other, trying to communicate telepathically to see if everyone agreed.

"You don't have to take me up on the offer. I mean, you've only just met me. These are dangerous times, and I'd understand completely if you didn't want to accept, but I just figured I would offer. I'm sorry you got robbed . . ."

"No, no," Karina answered. "I think I speak for all of us when I say we would love a ride to Vail."

The group looked back at Karina, unsettled that she would make the decision without consulting everyone. Janice noticed the hesitation on the other three, and shifted uncomfortably before responding. "It looks like maybe you all might want to discuss this amongst yourselves. So, if you guys want a ride, I'd be happy to give you one. I'm quite tired now, and will head to bed. My tent is about five tents away over there, so let me know what you guys decide. And thank you for the food. It was very kind."

"Do you want someone to walk you?" Jeremy asked.

"No, I'll be alright. I've been here two weeks already. I should be fine. Thank you, though."

6

TWO MOUNTAINS AND A WORLD AWAY

July 23, 2016
Los Alamos Research Laboratory

Suri and Robert sat in the conference room speaking to Dr. Ivanov, the nuclear physicist who had come from Russia to help stop the comet. He was a tall man, and well built. Robert thought he would make a good villain in a *Rocky* movie. Dr. Petrov was also in attendance—another Russian physicist—and so was Dr. Campero, a Chilean astronomer and expert in comets. Secretary Brighton and General Diaz, leader of the U.S. Armed Forces, sat in the background listening.

"Ve have ze use of ze American military . . . " Dr. Ivanov intoned.

"I agree," Robert replied, looking back to General Diaz.

"I vould also like to see zem in action," Dr. Petrov agreed.

"To do what, exactly?" General Diaz asked.

"Well," Robert explained to Secretary Brighton, "Chile is one of the best places in the world to view space. It has a very high elevation, and is extremely dry. Chile recently built something called the LSST, or Large Synoptic Survey Telescope, which will allow us to make short movies of the night sky. If we can gain access to it, we can train it on Shiva so we can look at it at all times. We'll basically have a live feed, which will be very important in projecting its trajectory toward Earth for precision targeting."

"Okay, so what's the issue? To my knowledge we were using this telescope already."

"We were, yes," Robert responded. "The problem now, is that it's not on. We need to turn it back on."

"On? What do you mean it's not *on*?"

Dr. Campero, the Chilean astronomer and one

of the scientists who had helped build the telescope, spoke up. "We lost contact with the telescope. This led us to believe that some anarchists in Chile may have purposefully disabled it. We believe the cabling that allows us to remotely move the telescope on its base rotationally has been cut. Basically, we can't follow the comet's path unless we fix this issue. We have to go there and fix it."

"There isn't someone working there now?" Secretary Brighton asked.

"Well, there was, but not since the Chilean Revolution. It seems like a local militia is trying to sabotage our plan," Robert replied angrily.

"What about the other telescopes? We have several pointed at the comet at all times, right? What makes this one special?" Secretary Brighton asked.

"Well," Dr. Campero responded, "the LSST will help us determine the comet's trajectory more accurately than the others. The more data we get on the comet's position, the better off we are."

I get that some people have lost hope, Robert thought

with dismay, *I just can't believe they would intentionally sabotage the equipment that's trying to save it.*

Secretary Brighton agreed that they needed to send a team to Chile, and said he would speak with the President and the Secretary of Defense as well.

"Where, exactly, is this telescope?" General Diaz asked Robert, looking up from his computer.

"It's on a plateau near the mountain Cerro Pachón, around sixty kilometers from the coastal city of La Serena," Dr. Campero replied.

After briefly consulting a map, General Diaz said gruffly, "There is an aircraft carrier currently within range of La Serena. I can assemble a team that can accompany Dr. Campero to the telescope, where he can fix it. Perhaps we ought to leave a team of soldiers stationed there to protect the telescope from future sabotage?"

"Good idea," Robert noted. "Oh, make sure you bring liquid nitrogen to the telescope. The CCDs will need to be cooled."

"Hold on a minute," Secretary Brighton said. "I'll need to speak with the Secretary of Defense."

General Diaz rolled his eyes, and Robert said, "Fine, but do it quickly. We need this telescope live ASAP."

Secretary Brighton nodded and got the approvals. Later that day, Dr. Campero was flown down to San Diego to meet SEAL Team Five, who would provide protection and help to get Dr. Campero to the telescope.

Early the next morning, Suri, Robert, Secretary Brighton, and General Diaz sat in a conference room watching the live feed of a helicopter as it left the USS Theodore Roosevelt and set off for Cerro Pachón. Secretary Brighton, who had served in Vietnam as a Captain in the Army, watched nervously as General Diaz gave commands to Captain Bergdan.

Robert and Suri both cupped warm cups of coffee. The team flew in just before dawn so they could have the cover of night.

Fortunately, as they flew in, there were no signs of

a militia near the telescope. Dr. Ivanov sighed audibly, evidently saddened he would have to wait for another day to see a Navy SEAL fight. Suri rolled her eyes at Dr. Ivanov.

Robert watched as the camera—which sat atop one of the officer's helmets—swiveled from side to side. He saw the side of the helicopter, then Dr. Campero looking nervous and awkward in a bulletproof vest, and then a menacing machine gun pointed at the LSST. They circled around and landed near it. Robert, who hadn't ever been to the LSST, marveled at its size, and then Dr. Campero turned over to the officer with the camera and spoke into the camera.

"I should have this figured out in a few hours, and I'll keep you updated on my progress."

"Thank you, Francisco," Robert replied.

Secretary Brighton turned off the sound to the television, and then asked for an update from Robert on the IMPs traveling toward the comet.

"They are on course; no issues for the moment. The first IMPs we launched will reach the comet in approximately one month. Coincidentally, the comet will be visible to the naked eye around that time too. This is when the comet's tail will become visible. The comet's ices will begin to sublimate, or turn into gas, and these gasses will be lit up by the Sun. Of the twenty missiles we have launched, twelve of them are nuclear. Of those twelve, nine are successfully on course for Shiva. The other two failed to launch, and we are working on fixing the failed thrusters. Of the eight observational satellites, there are also six heading successfully, which will help identify the comet's composition and track its movements."

Robert handed the Secretary a data sheet for the missiles. Then he took Secretary Brighton into the hallway, wanting to share the last piece of information alone. When they were outside, Robert began.

"There is one other thing that I haven't brought up with you yet . . ."

Secretary Brighton raised his eyebrows.

Robert told him about Gerald Jan and Vishnu,

the manned spacecraft due to orbit Shiva and help to defeat it.

"Jan . . . Jan . . . " Brighton repeated. "Isn't he the electric car guy?"

"Yeah, the billionaire. He retrofitted all his factories to help build this huge machine to help us save the world."

"And he didn't want to work directly for the United States?"

"You could say he's an individualist. He doesn't always trust governments."

"Ah . . . well, he sounds like a true American then," Secretary Brighton paused, thinking. "And you believe in this man? You trust in his design and his word?"

"I do, sir. I think having the Vishnu spacecraft could only help us. Jan told me yesterday that Vishnu would be ready to launch around eight months before the comet's estimated impact date. I think it would really help. But Jan does need something from us."

"And what is that?"

Robert gulped. "Sixteen nuclear weapons."

Secretary Brighton blanched.

"They can be short range," Robert countered quickly. "They would be traveling toward the comet from the orbiting Vishnu spaceship. I know the Joint Chiefs and possibly President Chaplin would consider this a huge threat to national security, but the Vishnu spaceship will make our survival a lot more likely."

"How much more likely?"

"Orders of magnitude, sir. It could save us."

Secretary Brighton paused again, rubbing his fingers on his chin before speaking. "All right, Dr. Miller. I'll do what I can to see if we can work together."

"Thank you, Mr. Secretary," Robert replied gratefully. "There is one more thing . . . about the hack by the Union Anarchists . . . the ones that may have been responsible for the Miami bombing. Have you gotten any more information?"

Secretary Brighton stared at Robert intently, as if considering if the information would help Robert work, and replied diplomatically, "We are investigating the evidence of a security breach by the Union

Anarchists to sabotage the IMP that detonated above Miami. We have classified them as a terrorist group, however, and are continuing to monitor their activities. We have taken measures to prevent any future attacks."

"Okay, thanks," Robert said, and unsatisfied by the answer, muttered, "I guess."

"Robert, the devastation in Miami was horrible. Tens of thousands dead; hundreds of thousands of casualties. It's just awful. And this is bound to reduce our capacity to save the world because we have lost some of the trust of our people. But we must soldier on; we must continue to build rockets and fight against the comet. We have no other choice, so please, don't lose hope," Secretary Brighton said, before they turned to go back to the conference room.

Suri looked up when Robert and Secretary Brighton reentered the conference room. Everyone was occupied while they waited for Dr. Campero to give an update regarding the LSST.

Brighton noticed Suri reading the papers in front

of her and asked, "How is our production rate for the nuclear weapons?"

"We are ahead of our projection, sir, and should have a healthy stockpile to continue bombing at our projected rate."

Launching all the rockets immediately would be irresponsible. If the comet's jets were to change unexpectedly, they might miss the comet entirely. And if its path did change slightly over time, they would have to recalibrate the missiles. As their data about the comet increased, they would know more specifically where to explode the nukes on the comet as well.

"I vant to mention that I spoke with the Minister of Defense of Russia, Sergei Medinsky," Dr. Petrov said, "and he is happy to say our rocket production is coming along as planned as vell."

Secretary Brighton nodded, still feeling a little odd about how the two former enemies were now working together as allies.

Robert and Suri had been splitting their time between the Los Alamos National Laboratory and the

Kennedy Space Center, and Robert had never had so much work on his plate.

As the lead scientist overlooking the entire project, he had to bring together all different types of scientists. There were the observing astronomers who worked out which telescopes to use, and at which times to use them. They were using optical telescopes to find out about the comet's spin and composition, and using radar telescopes to determine the comet's shape. The observers would turn their data over to the theoretical astronomers, who would create three-dimensional models of the comet, identifying its shape, spin, speed, and many other variables.

Then Robert had to work with the nuclear physicists, who were in charge of building the bombs. Their specifications were sent to the rocket scientists, who would send the bombs to the locations identified by the theorists. It was all enough stress to give Robert an ulcer, but he found ways to enjoy the little things—for example, the switching of the cafeteria and the engineering offices.

Since everyone had to work together, constantly giving feedback to each other, they all needed to be in the same room. The only room big enough was the cafeteria, so working together—like when the team of rocket scientists met with the team of theoretical astronomers—they were forced to go to the cafeteria to collaborate. Of course, if a few different engineering teams did this, it left almost no seats for people to eat, so they were forced to grab their food and sit in the small offices previously reserved for the engineers! Robert still worked in his office, but he often found himself visiting the cafeteria because so many of the engineers worked there. At least the coffee was always close by.

• • •

Jeremy woke up very hot. It was always like that when he camped; he would sleep until he felt like the tent was cooking him for breakfast. Anna was still fast asleep. Jeremy wiped the sleep from his groggy eyes and unzipped the tent, which was always louder than he expected. He stepped out of the tent, and his eyes adjusted. There were smoldering campfires all around the campsite, and it was completely quiet. The partiers had gone to bed, and a solitary car sat on the side of the road with its doors open. Jeremy could see Janice packing her things into the car, and his watch said it was already nine in the morning.

Dustin and Karina were already packing the tent in. Whatever had happened between them, they looked a lot more comfortable together. They looked happy.

"Hey guys, good morning!" Jeremy called.

"Howdy, man. Morning."

"Morning!" Karina added.

Jeremy helped them finish with the tent, and then woke up Anna.

"Five more minutes," she said, still asleep.

"Come on, Anna," Jeremy groaned.

"Let's go, girl! Time for us to get outta here!" Karina said, and grabbed Anna's leg, pulling at it.

"Ahhh," Anna whined, finally rubbing her eyes awake and peering out. "I hate you guys," Anna mumbled.

"So, what do you guys think? Should we go with Janice?" Dustin asked.

"It's better than staying here," Jeremy replied. "We are four, she's only one, so it's not like she can rob us. Plus I have the gun. If things get weird—like if she starts driving in the wrong direction—it wouldn't be hard to overpower her."

Karina nodded, adding, "I agree with Jeremy. It's better to go up north than stay with all these people."

One look around convinced the group this was true, so they decided to take Janice up on her offer. Once everything was packed up, they walked over to Janice's car and stuffed everything in the trunk.

The drive was beautiful, even though they were scrunched in the small Honda sedan. Jeremy sat in the front with his backpack on his lap, and the other three squeezed in the backseat. The drive was fast and Jeremy looked out the window so he wouldn't get carsick. *It would have been terrible to walk this distance,* Jeremy thought. The drive took them less than three hours. Once they got to Vail, it was another thirty minutes of windy roads and beautiful landscape until they made it. The cabin stood on a few acres of private property.

It was a large, two-story cabin. Anna excitedly ran up to it.

"I haven't been here in forever!" she called.

There was a large front porch complete with comfortable lawn chairs. The group got out of the car and stretched their legs, stiff from the packed car ride. Jeremy walked over forest floor to the cabin that was surrounded by huge pines, aspens, and firs. He walked inside the cabin to the living room and looked around. There was a built-in fireplace to the left, and a great brick chimney above it. The ceiling was tall and pyramidal, with a loft in the far corner. There was a staircase in the back of the cabin, which presumably went to the loft area. On the main floor, to the right, were three doors. Above the middle door loomed the stuffed head of a great buck. To the left was the kitchen. Anna ran out of the backdoor to turn on the generator, and within minutes the lights were all on.

"There are plenty of beds. Jeremy and I will take that one," Anna said, pointing to the far right door before continuing. "And Janice, you are welcome to stay with us until you figure out what you want to do."

"Thanks, Anna, that's so kind of you," Janice replied.

Jeremy grabbed his stuff from the car and put it in the room, then went back out to sit on the couch. He sighed in relief, sinking into the couch cushions. Finally they had made it to the cabin, where no one would hurt them, no one would steal their car, and where Anna would be safe. Dustin walked up the stairs to the loft and started rummaging around in a bookcase. Before long he said, "No way!" and ran back down the stairs.

"Check this out!" Dustin said, looking at Jeremy.

Dustin held an old *Playboy* magazine from the

1960's in his hands. He started to giggle when he saw the look of horror on Anna's face.

"Where did you find that?" Anna said, aghast.

"It's probably your dad's!" Jeremy said, laughing.

Anna chased Dustin around the room trying to snag the magazine from him, and Jeremy tried to block Anna from getting it. Then Jeremy got distracted, seeing something he'd forgotten existed—a landline phone. It was mounted on the wall with a long curly cord hanging down almost to the ground. He walked over and picked it up, then dialed his home number.

"Hello?" his father replied.

"Dad? Hi, it's Jeremy."

"Oh my God, it's you. Are you safe? Where are you? Your mother has been worried sick," Earl said quickly, and then yelled, "Karen! It's Jeremy. He's all right."

Jeremy heard a scream of relief come from his mother in the other room. He told his father the story of their drive. He left out the part where they got shot at and then carjacked at gunpoint.

"I'm sorry for leaving," Jeremy said, without thinking. Once the words got out of his mouth, however, he realized the rashness and the reckless nature of his decision to leave Houston without consulting his parents further.

"I'm so sorry, Dad," Jeremy repeated, and then heard his mother had picked up the living room phone. "And I'm sorry, Mom. I'm so sorry. I tried to tell you, I did, but I don't know, I—"

His mother interrupted him, "The important thing, honey, is that you're safe. You are safe, right?"

"Yes, Mom, I'm calling you from Anna's cabin in Vail. There are so few people here and we have a big stockpile of food and there's a river nearby for water. How is it in Houston?"

"It's getting worse here," his father replied. "There's a big terrorist group who are trying to take control. Maybe you've heard of them. They call themselves 'Union Anarchists.' They have begun spray painting all the road signs black, and beat up people on the side of the road. I don't really understand it. And now there are these fundamentalist Christian groups that are fighting with them, trying to take control themselves. They think the world is going to end and that everyone who isn't a believer is going to burn in . . . Ah, I should stop bothering you with this. How are you?"

Jeremy saw in the background that the others were desperate to call their parents as well.

"Hey Dad, listen, I gotta go. I think my friends want to call their parents to tell them they're safe too. Write down this number so that you can call me if you need to, and I'll talk to you soon, okay?" He gave his father the phone number.

"Okay, I love you."

"I love you, honey!" Jeremy's mother choked.

"Love you guys, too."

Jeremy found it was a lot harder to hang up the phone than he'd thought, but he managed to put the phone back on the receiver.

Karina walked up gingerly to where Jeremy stood, and he handed her the phone. The dial tone rang out, just barely audible in the spacious cabin. She dialed a number.

"Mom?" she asked.

7

THE NAVY SEALS
GET A NEW JOB

That same day . . .

While the conference room waited for Dr. Campero to figure out the problem with the LSST, the SEALs stood guard. Through a soldier's head camera, Suri saw graffiti on the wall of a small outbuilding that said, "*Juicio Final*," or "Final Judgment."

"Talk to me, Francisco," Robert called toward the screen in the conference room. He was staring at his computer, waiting for access to the LSST.

After another fifteen minutes, Dr. Campero appeared in front of the soldier with the camera.

"It should be working now, Robert," Dr. Campero replied. "Many of the cables had been cut through, but luckily most of them were just power cables. I forgot how much power this thing uses, and considering we haven't really used this telescope before—"

"Wait, what?" Secretary Brighton interrupted, glaring at Robert. "You've never used this telescope before? What do you mean? You just told me you'd been using it."

"Well," Robert answered, "construction was only recently completed. It hasn't really been used yet."

The Secretary fumed, "You mean to tell me this machine might not even help us?"

"Eit is our best chance, sir," Dr. Ivanov replied, "Ze LSST vill give us near-real-time footage, something zat no other telescope can give as accurately."

"This is what happens when you trust a bunch of scientists. All they want to do is play with the newest toys," the Secretary grumbled.

"Got it!" Dr. Campero exclaimed. "We should be good, Robert! Refresh the feed."

"Also, General Diaz, we are going to need some help from your SEAL team," Robert said slowly.

"What kind of help?" General Diaz replied suspiciously.

"Well, the CCDs—part of the imaging sensors— can get really hot, and the only thing that cools them and allows them to function is liquid nitrogen. Unfortunately, there's no working liquid nitrogen plant near Cerro Pachón. Dr. Campero made sure to take enough of it with him for at least a month, but after that . . . "

General Diaz was beside himself with anger. "These are the highest-trained soldiers in the entire Navy and you want to make them be pack-animals for you?" he asked incredulously.

"General Diaz, this is about saving the world. The Navy SEALs can't stop the comet from coming. What they can do is cool the equipment giving us the images that tell us the trajectory of the comet so we can blast the hell out of her."

General Diaz gave Robert a death stare, seething in silence.

Robert, feeling guilty about betraying Secretary

Brighton's trust, turned his attention to his laptop. He hit refresh on the screen, plugged in the access codes for the LSST, and waited.

"We are online!" he said.

Robert plugged in the projector to his computer, and the desktop appeared on the screen of one of the televisions.

"I'm going to program the LSST to stay tracked on Shiva. It may take a day before we have reliable data. This is a major breakthrough."

Robert looked around and saw Secretary Brighton looking curiously at him, nodding his head toward the door. Confused, he asked Suri to take over and excused himself.

"What's going on, Secretary? I'm sorry about misleading you about the LSST. It's just that we really need it."

Secretary Brighton looked more tired than usual and ignored Robert's apology. His customarily pristine suit was a bit wrinkled.

"An hour ago I got a call from the NSA Chief

and President Chaplin," he began. "It's about the Union Anarchists; they are gaining momentum. They have taken control of a few cities, including Denver, which we feel may be too close for comfort. We have reason to believe it was the same hacker, '@OneUnionAnarchist,' who hacked us again."

"Are you serious?"

"What I'm saying is, you need to be ready. For your safety and for the safety of what we are doing against the comet, we may need to relocate you and the team, probably to an island off the coast of Florida. It's a kind of safe house the government keeps, where you will be isolated from harm. It will also make trips to and from Cape Canaveral easier."

"These . . . Union Anarchists . . . do they understand that destroying the work we are doing would be killing our planet, our world, everything we care about? Everything they care about—assuming they care about anything at all!"

"It's maddening, I know. I'm not sure who leads this organization. President Chaplin and I believe that there might even be some members of Congress involved. But the Union Anarchists could be a cover, and to be honest, you need to focus on the engineering and astronomy, so try not to worry about this."

"Good God," Robert said, before asking again, "so Miami was a terrorist attack?"

"Yes," Brighton responded. "The NSA traced the IP addresses to a coffee shop in Denver. Then ChatSnap gave us all the photos and videos taken at that coffee shop in a four hour period, and we were able to piece together the perpetrator of the hack. We just don't know how deep this goes."

"ChatSnap gave you all their data?" Robert asked.

"Yeah. Well, since it's about national security, they had to. Robert, we can spy on any American we want."

"Wow. Why would the hackers want to end the world?" Robert repeated.

Secretary Brighton looked darkly at Robert, who tried unsuccessfully to decipher his gaze.

"That's what I need to find out. For now, just be ready to move at a moment's notice, and tell your scientists to prepare as well. Oh and Robert, do not ever, under any circumstances, lie to me about what you're doing again. We are trying to save the world here. Let's be on the same team, okay?"

Robert nodded, apologizing, and they walked back into the room together.

"What was that all about?" Suri asked. "That's the second time Brighton took you aside."

"I'll tell you later," Robert replied.

Back on the screen in Chile, Dr. Campero was making some adjustments to the LSST. Meanwhile, Captain Bergden notified General Diaz that he deployed a few SEALs on a recon mission toward the mountain town of Vicuña toward La Serena. They spotted a camp of soldiers with assault rifles occupying a section of the road between Vicuña and La Serena.

"Your orders, sir?" Captain Bergden asked.

"Defend the telescope," General Diaz replied. "Do not preemptively strike. From seeing the helicopter, they probably know where you are located, and possibly about the USS Roosevelt, but do not engage unless the telescope is threatened."

"Yes, sir."

"Also," General Diaz said through gritted teeth, "you will need to travel back and forth from the USS Roosevelt to bring tanks of liquid nitrogen. Follow Dr. Campero's instructions on how many tanks and what to do with them when you make it back to the telescope."

"Yes, sir."

8

THE ARK

August 3, 2016
Anna's Cabin

They had been at the cabin for a week. Jeremy sat on the floor of the loft, letting his feet dangle over its edge above the living room. "I Can't Stop" by Flux Pavilion was blaring on the stereo and the others were dancing below him. It was nine p.m., dirty dishes littered the tables around the cabin, and empty glasses were strewn about. Trash overflowed on the ground. They had done little more than hike around, make food, and shoot the hunting rifle they'd found at the cabin. Jeremy rubbed the stubble on his chin, watching Dustin and Karina, thinking they had become boyfriend and girlfriend. Jeremy couldn't tell whether it was for lack of options or because they genuinely liked each other.

"I can't stop!!" screamed everyone but Jeremy, laughing and dancing.

Jeremy swung his legs back down to the ground and walked over the blankets on the floor. He wasn't in the mood to dance. He went down the stairs and walked out into the crisp Colorado air. It was much colder outside than in the cabin and the air smelled like cold pine needles. He walked a ways to a clearing in the trees where he could see the stars. Jeremy tried to find the comet but didn't see anything, and sighed. He stood there for a few minutes in silence.

"Trying to find the comet?" Janice asked.

Jeremy jumped and looked to his left where Janice stood beside him.

"You scared me . . . but yeah, I was."

"I haven't been able to see it yet either, except that one grainy photo they showed us when the president delivered her speech."

They stood in silence for a while until Jeremy had an idea.

"Can I see it?" he asked.

"See what?"

"The Ark. When we first met you told us about that big ship that was being built in the Rockies. Is it close to here?"

Janice was silent again for a moment.

"Um, yeah, sure. Why do you want to see it?"

"I'm just curious. Not that I think what they're doing is really that cool, but building something that could orbit Earth for a while would be awesome. Pretty sweet engineering, you know?"

Janice laughed. "Pretty sweet engineering," she repeated. "Yeah, that's one way to put it. Well, I don't see why not."

"I mean, it's not dangerous to see it, right?"

"They'll have some patrols around, but it should be fine. I know of somewhere we can go and get a good view, but not more than that . . . Hey!"

Suddenly tensing up, Janice pointed down a path, but it was too dark.

Jeremy squinted his eyes, but saw nothing. "What is it?" he asked.

"Shhh!" Janice said quickly.

Jeremy looked harder and his heart started racing. About fifty yards in front of them a huge black bear slowly walked between the trees. The bear didn't seem to notice there were two humans standing so close to her, watching her majestic wildness. The bear's shoulder blades stuck out as she moved—too quietly for her weight—through the forest.

"What should we do?" Jeremy whispered.

"We should stand here and wait, not talk, and try not to make sudden moves."

They watched in tranquil silence as the bear passed by, not noticing—or ignoring—them, and went along her way. Jeremy looked over at Janice, who had a curious look on her face, and stepped closer to him.

"I think we should get some sleep," Jeremy stuttered, afraid and amazed at the beautiful bear.

"I agree."

The next day, Jeremy and Janice spent the day organizing the food situation at the cabin. The cabin had a lot of cured meats and canned vegetables, not to mention pounds of rice. Anna's grandfather had been a bit scared of the nuclear winter the Cold War could have brought, so their cabin was stocked full of food.

"Wake up, wake up!" Jeremy called.

"Not so loud, man," Dustin returned from the couch.

Jeremy cooked the last of their eggs and some steak he had found in the freezer. Soon, the smell of Jeremy's cooking woke everyone up, and Jeremy announced his plan to visit the Ark.

"That sounds a little dangerous," Anna said. "You talked about this with Janice?"

Jeremy really wanted Anna to come, but didn't want to start a "relationship" fight in front of everyone. *Women are so confusing*, he thought, *does she just want to party all the time until the world ends?*

"It'll be fun. And plus we'll probably get to

backpack for a day or two to reach a safe spot where we can see the Ark," Janice offered, and Anna shot her a look Jeremy couldn't decipher.

"Karina, what do you think?" Anna asked.

"I'm not too into it, but you guys can definitely go!"

"I'll stay behind and make sure Karina is okay," Dustin said, winking at Jeremy.

"So, looks like it's just us three?" Jeremy asked, hopeful that Anna would come as well.

"I'll go."

"You don't have to if you don't want to."

"No, it's fine. I want to go."

They all sat there picking at their food, except Dustin and Karina, who ate voraciously.

After breakfast, the trio packed up, and Karina let Janice use her backpacking backpack. As Jeremy packed his bag, Dustin pulled him aside.

"So Janice . . . " Dustin said, adopting a knowing smile.

"What about her?"

Dustin nodded and nudged him with his elbow.

"Dude, what are you talking about?"

"Nothing, man," Dustin laughed. "Forget it."

"You sure you don't want to come with us?"

"Yeah. I mean it sounds fun, but staying here with Karina sounds fun too. Coming to the cabin was such a good idea!"

He hugged his best friend, and walked out to the car.

"I'll see you when we get back, man."

Once inside the car, Janice started the engine and drove north. She took so many turns that eventually Jeremy had no idea where he was. He was momentarily nervous that this was a trap—that somehow they were needed for some plan by the über-rich, and Janice was their undercover agent posing as a friend.

This feeling did not go away once it made its way into Jeremy's mind. It only grew, and when they stopped in front of a dark trailhead, it grew worse.

"Ready?" Janice asked.

"How far do you think it is?" Anna inquired.

"Not sure, but we'll definitely have to camp for a night, maybe two. Let's just hope we don't spot any bears," Janice said, winking at Jeremy.

It took them one full day to reach the valley where Janice said the Ark was being built. The night was freezing and the backpacks were heavy, but there was a stream that tumbled out of the mountain, so at least they had access to drinkable water. In the morning, they ate beans and rice, which were rapidly becoming their only source of food. Jeremy figured that soon they would need to go hunting.

The trio talked about the United States and what they thought was happening around the country while they walked. Janice told them about the Union Anarchists, who had assumed control of much of Denver. The Union Anarchists were a group of people who wanted to see the world crumble, and who felt that there was no reason for living. At the helm was a philosopher—a man identified only as Mr. K—who argued that the comet was too large to move by any force. He said that the coming of the comet proved that there was no God, and told the people to join him in anarchy, and in living without rules, without bureaucracy, without the rule of law.

"If you guys had gone any farther into Denver," Janice said, "you would have noticed the slogan: Live Until Death, or L.U.D. It's all over the town now. Some people are even getting tattoos of the slogan. That's another reason why I was in Denver—I wanted to see what the Union Anarchists were about. There is so much going on that none of us know about, that I felt I should do a little firsthand research. Well, I was not impressed."

"Did you ever meet their leader, Mr. K?" Anna asked.

"No, but I saw him speak once through a black-market TV station. He was only a silhouette, and he wore a bowler hat, which I thought was weird."

"What did he say?"

"Oh, the usual. Take up our cause, their cause sucks, that kind of thing."

They were slowly climbing over the pass, which was largely covered by trees.

"It should only be another half hour. We should keep as quiet as possible now."

This is so stupid, what are we doing? Jeremy thought to himself, realizing that he'd wanted to get away from danger by going to Vail. Suddenly, partying in Anna's cabin and relaxing with Dustin and Karina seemed like a great idea. They were slowly climbing down the mountainous path when Janice stopped the group by raising her right hand. Jeremy tried to peer through the trees but couldn't make out too much, so they crept closer. The group put their backpacks down, hiding them behind two bristlecone pines, and continued.

"What were we trying to accomplish here, again?" Anna whispered to Jeremy.

"I don't remember . . . " Jeremy whispered.

They moved on. The valley was very deep, and finally they came to a small area, just wide enough to punch a golf ball through, where they could peer down through the trees. The Ark looked impossibly large to go into space, especially from the rockets he'd seen leave Cape Canaveral on the news.

It seemed like the hardest thing about space travel was getting far enough away from Earth's gravity, and this thing was huge. The ship looked absolutely immense. And it did look like something from *Star Wars*. In the middle of the hulking mass of metal was a huge rectangular glass—at least Jeremy thought it was glass; it was transparent—and he could see plants inside. They crept closer and Jeremy saw that the ship contained what looked like a huge spinning wheel, like a hamster wheel. In a book he once read, he had seen sketches of something similar. It was used to create artificial gravity, but as far as Jeremy knew it had never been done outside of science fiction books.

"Jeremy, look!"

Jeremy snapped out of his reverie, and below the gigantic spaceship, five small dots were making their way toward the thicket of trees where they stood.

"What should we do?" Anna asked.

Jeremy remembered that he had packed a pair of binoculars in his backpack, so he sprinted back to where he left it.

"What are you doing?" Janice hissed.

"Jer, you serious right now?" Anna said almost at the same time.

Jeremy slid in next to his backpack and began rifling through it, finally finding the binoculars in the side pocket. He took them out and ripped them out of the packaging and returned to the place Janice and Anna were waiting. He put the lenses to his eyes and adjusted the focus.

"They have guns," he said.

"We should probably go then . . . " Anna said nervously.

Janice was the first to go and Anna followed, but Jeremy hesitated. They had a good head start on these mysterious figures; running away didn't make sense. *We can't just outrun them,* Jeremy thought. *We are a full day away from the car; they'll easily catch up to us . . .*

"Guys, wait!" Jeremy called.

Anna and Janice looked back.

"What?" Janice called. "Are they getting closer?"

"No! Well maybe, I don't know! That's the point. Will you just stop running for a second?"

They did, and Jeremy replied, "Thanks. I think we should make sure they are actually following us."

Anna knew what to do. She looked around quickly and found a low-lying branch attached to one of the larger white pine trees. She grabbed it and pulled herself up, and Jeremy threw the binoculars toward her. She caught them, slung them around her neck, and headed up.

"Impressive," Janice said to Jeremy.

Jeremy felt a little inexplicable pride toward his girlfriend at how fast she climbed. If they made it an Olympic sport, she would win the gold. Within two minutes she was at the top—so high that the wind swayed the tree precariously back and forth.

"Be careful!" Jeremy called, hoping his voice wouldn't arouse suspicion.

She scanned in every direction for about a minute before heading back down, taking care to step firmly on each branch. Jeremy caught her when she jumped from the last branch to the forest floor.

"They didn't even go into the forest," she said, brushing the pine's sticky needles off her shirt. "They just aimed their guns into the trees and looked a bit. Then they walked back. The view up there was amazing, though. The spaceship—the Ark—is truly remarkable. That circular contraption, what is that for?"

"I think it's for artificial gravity," Jeremy replied. "There's something I don't quite get," he said, looking at Janice. "With the drag from the atmosphere, it's going to be difficult to get it into space, right?"

"You're right, Jeremy. It is for artificial gravity, but they'll deconstruct it and reconstruct it in space, so they don't have to worry about the drag."

"So they really are going to do it," Jeremy said. "They're really just going to leave Earth behind?"

"Just until the literal 'dust' settles on the planet after impact. Then they'll return."

"Why aren't you with them?" Anna asked.

Janice paused. "It's just wrong. They're greedy and selfish, leaving Earth when they have the resources to help try to save it. One of them even told me the comet was a blessing—that the Earth would be saved from the overpopulation problem. Isn't that disgusting?"

Jeremy didn't answer, and they decided to return to the cabin. They hiked back down the mountain and toward the car, reaching it just before dark. Jeremy felt a strange sensation in his mind as he thought about the huge Ark being sent into space. *What am I doing?* he thought. *I'm living out my last years like the anarchists, just waiting to die, when I could be helping.* After what Janice said, he wondered if she felt the same way.

When they returned to the cabin, they found Karina and Dustin making dinner.

"Right on time," Karina called. "Oh and Anna, your mom called. Can you call her back?"

"Oh! Yes, thanks Karina."

As Jeremy set the table and excitedly told Dustin what he'd seen, Anna spoke in hushed tones on the phone. When she returned, she made an announcement.

"My parents have decided to join us in the cabin!" she exclaimed.

"No more partying?" Dustin asked in dismay.

They were set to come in a few weeks' time.

9

AN OLD VOICE

August 16, 2016
Los Alamos National Laboratory

Robert sat in the conference room with Suri and Secretary Brighton at his side. A haggard President Chaplin sat waiting for the most recent developments in the fight against Shiva.

"With LSST, we now have a daily near-live feed of the comet," Robert began. "Through a combination of three-dimensional modeling based on the optical, radio, and x-ray spectroscopy from the observational scientists, Dr. Campero's team has found the weakest points of the comet. We have identified two main locations to target, and have set the course for our IMPs to detonate at these locations."

"When will this occur?" President Chaplin asked.

"Unfortunately, Madam President, because the comet is still outside Saturn's orbit, our IMPs won't be able to reach the comet for another six months."

"I see in your notes here that the speed of the comet will change. How?"

"According to Kepler's Law of Orbits, all orbiting bodies move faster the closer they are to the body they are orbiting," Suri explained. "The photographs taken by the LSST and other telescopes are giving us tons of data to mine through and discover new things about the comet. For example, yesterday I found out that the comet comes from a special region of the Kuiper Belt where—"

"Excuse me," President Chaplin chided. "But you are looking at where the comet came from? Shouldn't you be more focused on where it's going?"

"Where it came from gives us a better indication of its composition," Suri explained, unaffected by the president's interruption. "Things that are in the same area in the Kuiper Belt tend to be similar in composition."

"The closer the comet comes, the more accurate we will be, and the more nuclear weapons we will use. As you can see here," Robert said, pulling up some photos on his computer, "we are also monitoring our IMPs as they fly through space toward the comet."

President Chaplin looked over the photos on her own computer and said, "This is good work, Dr. Miller. Thank you. Is there anything else?"

"Well," Robert replied enthusiastically, "we've made two big discoveries about the comet. Firstly, as Suri was stating, we learned a lot more about the composition. We've learned of a massive pocket of gaseous ammonia just under the comet's surface. It's a perfect target for our nuclear weapons."

"Why is it perfect?"

"Well, the surface of the comet just over the pocket is thin enough that we can expose the pocket to space. The gas will then slowly trickle out of the comet, allowing us to begin diverting the comet."

"Excellent, and secondly?"

"Our nuclear and rocket scientist team designed a nuclear-powered rocket that could decrease the travel time of the IMPs, but this would mean increasing our production of weapons-grade plutonium."

Immediately in the conference room, there were objections to adding nuclear weapons to the IMPs, especially since Miami was so fresh in everyone's mind.

"I don't know if we can allow that," Secretary Brighton said.

"I know Miami was devastating," Robert said, "and that the public will be unhappy about this possibility, but using oxygen fuel was fine in the beginning. We need to get more IMPs on their way to the comet, and nuclear-powered rockets will help. We already use nuclear power for submarines, and honestly, the impact of another failure would be just as devastating with or without this addition."

Everyone was silently watching the screen where President Chaplin was deep in thought.

"Okay, start work on these nuclear-propelled

rockets, but I want to be kept one hundred percent in the loop about this project," President Chaplin finally said. "Now," she said, changing the subject, "due to the recent security breaches and attacks, in the coming month we will be relocating your entire team to an undisclosed location to ensure your safety."

Suddenly, Robert felt his pocket buzz. It was his cell phone, which he quickly silenced.

"I've also spoken with Secretary Brighton, and I am green-lighting the project with Gerald Jan. Please do whatever you can to help him. We now have just under two years before the comet arrives and . . . "

Robert immediately looked back to his computer to the plans created by the nuclear scientist team working on the integration of the nukes to the Vishnu spaceship. Then his mind drifted back to his cell phone. Aside from the people in the room, he could only remember giving that number to his daughter. He hadn't heard from her for a few weeks. He thought about her every day, hoping she was safe, hoping she would reach the cabin or find some other shelter.

His daughter's safety was of paramount importance to him, yet he could do nothing to help her. It was agonizing. He had to stay focused on the much larger problem. His only hope was saving the world from the comet, and in the process, save his daughter. When the meeting adjourned, Robert listened to the voicemail that Jennifer had left.

"Hey Dad, I hope you're doing well saving the world. I was hoping to hear your voice, but I'll leave this message. Isabel and I are safe at the cabin, but it took a lot longer to get here than we thought. We decided to go through Grand Junction and hit Vail from the west instead of the east, because we heard Denver was unsafe. Anyway, around one hundred miles away from the cabin, we ran out of gas. None of the gas stations around had gas, and so we had to walk the rest of the way. We're all okay. Even little Isabel made it. Anyway, now you have this number if you want to get in contact for any reason, and . . . well, I just wanted to say I love you. And good luck."

Robert listened to the message three times before

putting the phone back into his pocket. Robert was supposed to view a rocket leaving from Cape Canaveral—a test for the upcoming bombardment—so he made his way to the Situation Room. As he walked with Suri, he was aware that she did not know where her parents were or how they were doing. The last she had heard, they had gotten on one of the last flights to New Delhi and were hoping to return to their home village. Robert wished there was some way he could help her, and then his phone started to buzz again.

Annoyed, Robert answered the phone.

"What?"

"Dr. Miller?"

"Who's this?"

"This is Jeremy Genser, sir. You gave me your phone number before I left Houston . . ."

"Jeremy, of course! I'm sorry. I assume you made it to your girlfriend's cabin?"

"Yes, I did, and I wanted to apologize for not checking up on your daughter. I tried the phone number you gave me but Jennifer never picked up the phone."

"I actually just got a voicemail from her. She is all right," Robert said. "Is that why you called?"

"Well, sir, I've been thinking a lot, and I wanted to call you to ask if there was anything I could do to help in the effort against the comet? It doesn't feel right just living my days out in this cabin while there are other people trying to save the world. I want to help in any way that I can. I know I'm not the most qualified or experienced person, but if there is anything at all I can do, please let me know." Jeremy hung on the other line, holding his breath.

Suri looked at Robert quizzically, wondering who he was talking to. Robert frowned, thinking for something a trustworthy high school student could do to help stop a big ball of ice and rock from hitting Earth.

"I need to think, Jeremy. As of now I can't think of much. I will, though, just sit tight. I can call you at this number?"

"Yes, you can."

"Good, then stay put for now. I'll call you back as soon as I think of something."

Suri and Robert continued walking, and Dr. Campero came up behind them.

"Robert, can I speak with you?"

"I'm just on my way to the Situation Room for some testing. What is it, Francisco?"

"The current projections for our bombardment rate. I spoke with Dr. Suarez about Shiva's composition and structural integrity. We think that considering a gravitational-pull method might be more successful."

Robert considered for a moment before replying. "You think that we might split the comet up. Break her in half, maybe?"

"Or more than half. I don't know; it seems risky."

"A gravitational-pull method could help the comet, but we don't have enough time to send an object massive enough," Suri answered. "There is no other choice, don't you agree, Dr. Campero? If Shiva falls apart from our bombing, then we'll regroup and adjust, but we can't risk its entire mass hitting us."

Francisco tried ignoring Suri, but Robert was shaking his head at him.

"Listen to Dr. Lahdka, Francisco. If we had maybe four years, we'd have more options. Direct and indirect bombardment is what we have to do."

Dr. Campero looked at them both, snorted, and walked in the opposite direction away from the meeting.

Suri and Robert both decided to ignore the behavior and continued to the situation room. The gravitational pull method was simple enough. Launch massive objects to one side in order to use gravity to pull the comet away from a collision course with Earth. However, it was too costly, and Robert feared it wouldn't work in time to move the comet out of the way before the expected collision date.

10

THE WAITING GAME

September 1, 2016
Anna's cabin

Jeremy sat next to the corded phone hanging on the wall. He was anxiously waiting for it to ring, but to his dismay, Dr. Robert Miller hadn't called yet. He felt helpless, restless, hopeless. Even if he was safe from the increasingly anarchic United States, being at the cabin was wearing on his mental health. When he'd called his parents, they said that they were scared of going out at night, and their house had been broken into three times.

"I'm just happy you're safe up there in Vail," Earl had said.

Jeremy didn't tell him how boring it had become.

The first few weeks had been great—like a vacation. No school, wake up whenever you want, and Jeremy could go hiking and exploring around some of the most beautiful nature in the Western Hemisphere. However, he often found himself looking up toward the sky, wondering if he was just wasting his time. He longed for excitement.

Shiva, although still invisible, was up there in the sky somewhere, a constant reminder of the world's end. In the two weeks since he had called Robert saying he wanted to help, he had returned to the huge spaceship built by billionaires—the Ark. He had wanted to take some photos and see it again, maybe get closer.

He went with Dustin and Karina, and this time they got closer to the ship. They hadn't seen any guards around the base of it, but there were some large cabins, if you could call them cabins, on the hillside opposite the clearing. The cabins looked more like big log mansions—like something the Yeti would live in.

"It's huge," Karina gasped when she saw the Ark.

Dustin agreed, but all three of them were too scared to go any farther and explore around the base of the ship, even though it looked deserted.

"It doesn't have wings," Dustin remarked. "Shouldn't it have wings?"

"It's not really a spaceship; it's more like a big satellite," Jeremy explained. "It'll launch and begin orbiting Earth, so it just needs to be aerodynamic enough to get through the atmosphere."

Jeremy found the second time looking at the rocket meant he could take in its prodigious magnificence more clearly. There were nine gargantuan inverted cones on the bottom of the ship, which was where the exhaust came out.

"Aren't they going to come back down again?" Karina asked. "Will this land?"

"I'd guess they'd have a bunch of escape pods and land in the ocean or something," Jeremy mused.

"If the ocean still exists, right? I mean, what if the comet just hits it so hard that all its water is moved . . . " Dustin considered bleakly.

"Weird," Karina said, as she looked up at the tip of the rocket. "If somehow we do escape out of this mess alive and see the world after, it's crazy to think it could look nothing like it does now . . . "

When they headed back toward the car, Karina walked ahead and Dustin hung back to walk alongside Jeremy.

"So I wanted to talk to you about something," Dustin began.

"What's up, D?"

"Well, you know that Karina and I have been, well, seeing each other recently."

"I guessed that."

Dustin laughed nervously before continuing. "Well, right after you spoke to Dr. Miller about helping out, Karina and I started a little plan of our own. We want to go to Europe."

Jeremy started to laugh, but then stopped when he saw Dustin's emotionless expression, and asked, "What? You're not joking?"

"We decided that now would be a better time than any to travel, since there's not much time left, right?"

"Right . . . but Dustin, how could you possibly get to Europe? Commercial flights aren't available."

"I know, but I spoke to Janice, and she said that if we can get to Houston then we can get on a boat going back with some supplies to a place called Rotterdam, which is in The Netherlands. I just wanted to ask you a question."

"Is it, 'Do I think this is a stupid idea?'"

"No . . . do you trust Janice?"

Jeremy thought for a spell, knowing this was the moment where he would be able to do everything in his power to change his friend's mind; all he had to do was fabricate some story about why not to trust Janice Effran, the woman they had only known for six weeks, and Dustin would stay. Jeremy looked up at the sky as they walked, thinking about the comet, and decided.

"I trust her, Dustin. Do what makes you happy."

They walked for a time in silence.

"What do you think you'll do if that scientist doesn't call you back?"

"I'll call him again, or I'll call the government hotline number and work in a factory or something . . . When would you leave?"

"I'm not sure. Probably soon, though. Enjoy the mountains a bit more, you know, and then start walking. Enough time has passed; maybe the anarchy is bad enough that we can find a car somehow, or pay someone if money still works."

"I agree, man. And there's always food, or other ways to pay aside from money. I didn't think that would happen, but now it's kind of crazy. I feel like I wasted too much time up here already."

When they got back home, Jeremy went to the bathroom and then watched Karina and Dustin play a game of chess.

"Jeremy!" Anna snapped from the bathroom.

Dustin and Karina stopped playing. Karina looking alarmed, but Dustin wore a sarcastic smile.

"What's up, Anna?" Jeremy asked, walking toward her.

Anna had her arms folded and looked visibly tense and annoyed.

"Go into the bathroom," she commanded.

Jeremy tried not to roll his eyes. "I left the seat up, didn't I? I don't get why this is such a big deal for you . . . "

Anna groaned and stormed off to the bedroom. Jeremy followed, and the argument descended from there. Jeremy argued that both men and women use the toilet, so it's up to the individual to use it how they like. He knew it was an age-old argument, as old as the toilet itself, but one that somehow the woman has, and always will, win. Only this time, the argument got so bad that at one moment, Anna burst into tears.

Worried, Jeremy closed the door. "What's going on? This is such a dumb argument. Can we just relax a little bit?"

Anna's face turned into a deep scowl. *Well,* Jeremy thought to himself, *that was the wrong thing to say.*

Jeremy spent the next hour trying to calm her down, saying things like, "I'm sorry," and, "Listen, I was wrong." The trouble was that he had no idea what he did wrong. He knew it was about more than just the toilet seat, but for the life of him couldn't figure out what. He even thought about it as he curled up on the couch that night, falling asleep feeling a familiar empathy for the men of the world—confusion about the fairer sex.

Jeremy awoke to the phone ringing near his ear. He rubbed his eyes and picked it up.

"Hello?"

"Jeremy, it's Dr. Miller."

"Oh, hi! How are you? What time is it?"

"Oh yeah, I figured I would wake you. It's around four in the morning. I have something I would like you to do."

"Name it!" Jeremy replied excitedly.

"Project DJD is moving to a new location and I need someone on the ground in Houston I can trust. There have been some whisperings about aristocratic billionaires planning their own project in regards to Shiva. I don't know enough about it yet, but I need to meet with you. Can you meet me on Friday in Houston? The bar that we visited together?"

Aristocratic billionaires . . . oh I have some news for you, Jeremy thought.

"Sure, sounds good."

"And Jeremy."

"Yes?"

"Be careful."

Jeremy hung up the phone, exhilarated, and found that it was difficult to fall back asleep. He tried packing in the dark, and turned on a flashlight. He went into the room and got some clothes, his backpacking backpack, and some road essentials. He almost laughed out loud when he found inside his backpack one of the rolled up *Playboy*s that Dustin had packed in the car. It seemed so long ago that they had left Texas in the Acura and the U-Haul.

By five in the morning he was ready to go. It was

still dark, so Jeremy settled back on the couch and fell asleep.

Jeremy woke up nervous; he was always nervous right before a trip. *And I still have to talk to Anna.*

"I think you should go," Anna said, when he entered her room and found her curled up in bed, holding a pillow in front of her body.

I didn't even tell her I was going to leave, Jeremy thought.

"I wish it didn't have to be like this," Jeremy said.

"Just go. That's what you want, right? It's boring here? You want to go save the world?"

"I'm not!" Jeremy said, but his voice lacked conviction.

"So, this is it then," Anna said. "We're breaking up."

"Maybe we should take a little break . . . "

Jeremy stood at the edge of the bed, looking at Anna, feeling suddenly very sad. He didn't know what else to say, and Anna turned her back to him, falling back to sleep—or pretending to at least. Jeremy walked out of the room, his head low. Dustin and Karina were making some breakfast—rice, lentils, kidney beans, and canned peas and carrots, being healthy by necessity.

He sat down to breakfast and ate quietly alongside Karina, Dustin, and Janice.

"So, Dr. Miller called me back, and asked me to work for him in Houston. So, after two months here, I think I'm going back to Texas."

"The scientist who is working to stop the meteor?" Janice asked, pricking her ears up.

"*Comet*," Jeremy, Dustin, and Karina said in unison.

Janice blinked at them all for a moment. "Right, comet."

"And Janice, I talked to Karina and I think we will take you up on that offer to go to Europe. We'll happily work on the shipping container."

They ate in silence again, trying not to address the elephant in the room. Finally, unable to stand it, Jeremy broke the silence with a comforting lie.

"Anna's okay with it. She wants me to go help Dr. Miller."

The others went with the lie to reduce the awkwardness, which Jeremy appreciated.

"Aren't her parents due to arrive any day?" Janice asked. She felt it would be a bit awkward to stay alone with Anna, and had decided to see about working in one of the government factories helping make the rockets.

Dustin, Janice, and Karina said goodbye to Anna while Jeremy waited in the car. He couldn't gather the courage to say goodbye again. Jeremy looked down at his shirt. It was the same one he had worn for a week now—a small plain black T-Shirt. It had stains all over it, mostly from ketchup, and a few holes from climbing trees. He still had his gun tucked in the back of his pants.

They started driving with Janice at the wheel. They drove quietly, and Jeremy looked out the window at the beautiful landscape passing him by. They made good time and decided this time not to stop in Denver, until Jeremy gasped.

"The U-Haul!" he remembered.

"What?" Janice asked.

"We could get the supplies from the U-Haul. We hid it in Denver on our way to Vail."

"Let it go, Jer," Karina replied. "It's too dangerous to go back."

"Aw, man," Dustin joked, "My *Playboys* were in there!"

As Karina rolled her eyes, Jeremy looked back at the Rocky Mountains which were getting smaller behind them.

"Yeah, I guess you're right," he said, as they made their way back to civilization.

The signs around Denver were newer. There were several UA tags, and there were even UA tags on the freeway concrete.

"United Airlines is really going for a new advertising campaign, aren't they?" Dustin laughed.

"Too lame, man," Jeremy commented.

Above them, the comet hurled savagely toward them, and below them the concrete sped by. It looked like the mysterious Union Anarchists were expanding. Jeremy had yet to meet one of these people, though perhaps the ones to steal his car had been agents of the group. Jeremy fell into a tumultuous sleep as their small sedan sped along the pavement, south toward Houston.

11

SOUTH

September 2, 2016
Near Raton, New Mexico

Incredibly, the drive back to Houston was fairly uneventful. They found a gas station just when they reached New Mexico, and to Jeremy's surprise no one was there. He called into the mini-mart but there was no one. He looked; there were great big UA graffiti signs everywhere.

"Maybe the anarchists believe in free gas for all," Jeremy mused to himself.

He looked around the mini-mart and saw the shelves were all empty. Seeing no one, he walked in. One lonely bag of chips left on one shelf was just wishing to be grabbed and eaten. Unfortunately, it was

Sour Cream & Onion, a flavor that Jeremy absolutely detested. All the cigarettes behind the counter were gone.

He walked around the counter, and to his surprise saw the computer on, with sticky notes pasted to the side of the screen. The stickers told him the steps to allow a cash purchase for gasoline, so he did it. He felt a little guilty not paying for the gas, and it eased his conscience a bit when he opened the register to find that it was empty. Then he remembered he didn't have any cash anyway.

Jeremy took the nozzle and pumped up. Then he took the spare canisters they had in the car and filled those up as well. Jeremy, one hand on his pistol, scanned all around the gas station until the canisters were full. They figured with all their fuel canisters they would have enough to get back to Houston without having to pump again.

As they drove, it was apparent they were leaving the territory of the Union Anarchists. The graffiti had almost completely changed into religious fanaticism.

The roads in north Texas always displayed the numerous billboards of dead fetuses, Devil's pitchforks, and "Jesus Lives" messages, but things had become even more preposterous since they'd left. At every mile was a makeshift graffiti sign warning of the coming apocalypse. Jeremy read, "Don't stop the Apocalypse, Ascend to Heaven." Another one read: "Stop Devils Stopping the Apocalypse. Call 800-GOHEAVN." Jeremy shuddered, wondering who would answer.

He saw similar sentiments painted on the tops of houses as he drove by. He wondered if this was the threat Dr. Miller was talking about, if the threat to their work would come from religious fanatics. Considering what he knew about the current events of the past twenty years, he couldn't see why not. Religious fanaticism seemed like the most likely candidate to mess up any plan to save the world.

After crossing into Texas, they listened on the radio for any news about the world, and Jeremy's fears were realized. Several religious groups were talking about trying to stop the government from stopping Shiva. They said it was playing God.

"What I don't get," Jeremy began, "is that the government was able to shut down the entire internet. No Facebook, no Instagram, but we can hear on the radio about how the Christian Right wants to let the world get destroyed? Seems weird, right?"

"You're forgetting," Dustin replied, "that the internet can be easily controlled, but to broadcast a radio signal, all you need is a big radio tower and you're set. The people we just heard, they are most likely less than a hundred miles away from us right now." Jeremy suddenly realized he hadn't told his parents that he was leaving. *I'm a bad son. I should've told them a lot more . . .*

In contrast to northern Texas and Denver, Houston looked very similar to before Jeremy had left.

Janice drove the whole way, which impressed the rest of the group. She drove all the way to the Port of Houston, and headed for the ship that was going to Rotterdam.

"How did you find out about this again?" Karina asked a little nervously.

"So the Ark gets a lot of equipment and a lot of the world's richest families are from Europe, especially Russia. This is the ship they have been using to send the bulk of materials, personal belongings, and people across the Atlantic. They basically don't have anything to send back, so they sell the space to other enterprises, so there is always a need for people to clean and manage the cargo," Janice explained.

"Okay," Karina said, sounding nervous.

Dustin reminded Karina in a hushed voice that she'd wanted to see the churches in Europe. Their whispered conversation interspersed with hugs, then more whispers, made Jeremy feel like he was intruding. He tried to give them some space but it was impossible in the small car. Janice turned up the radio, which spoke more about the coming apocalypse.

"Well, you guys going to go or what?" Jeremy asked.

"Yes!" Karina said, finally excited.

The Port of Houston was a bustling scene, with people shouting orders at each other, dockworkers running around, and goods being rapidly loaded and unloaded from ships by huge cranes. The port ran remarkably smoothly. It was almost as if none of the workers felt the world was ending; their world moved along just as planned.

Dustin and Karina stepped out of the car, putting on their backpacks. Janice went to speak with a lead dockworker. He had a radio in his ear and seemed to be directing much of the foot traffic. Jeremy sat and waited, a bit unsure of how to say goodbye to his friends.

"I still can't believe you're just going to go," he admitted. "It feels like you're just doing this to do one more crazy thing. You know, we might be able to save the world here."

"And it might end too, but at least this way I'll be able to see Stonehenge and the cave paintings at Lascaux," Dustin replied.

"I never knew you were into history like that."

"I don't know, I think when I realized that I might never see that stuff, it became a lot more important. I've always wanted to see it before I died, and now, why not, you know?"

Jeremy could understand where his friend was coming from, but to end their lives while traveling the world as a tourist instead of working to save it was not something he would do.

He spoke up again. "And Karina, is that what you want to see, too? Dustin mentioned you wanted to see the churches, right?"

"That's right," Karina replied. "I want to see the Vatican. It has always been a dream, and then eventually we will try to make it to Jerusalem."

"I have to admit that it does sound pretty fun. I know it'll probably be impossible, but if there's any way you can get word to me on how you are doing and what you've been up to, I'd love to hear from you!"

"Of course, my friend!" Dustin exclaimed. "Right

when I find a phone, telegram, or post office, you'll be the first person that I'll reach out to!"

Jeremy took turns hugging both of them, and then they walked together to Janice, who had called them over to speak with the dockworker. He immediately sent them aboard a ship called the *SS Hamilton*, en route to Rotterdam, the Netherlands.

As Jeremy longingly watched Karina and Dustin step aboard the ship, he had a panging wish to return back to Colorado to be with Anna.

• • •

"You sure this is where you want me to drop you off?" Janice asked, looking nervously around the seedy Houston neighborhood.

"Yeah, Janice, thanks. I appreciate it. We can meet up tomorrow, maybe?"

"Sounds good, Jeremy. I'll keep in touch. Thanks for everything."

Janice kissed Jeremy on the cheek and Jeremy got

out of the car in the Third Ward. He walked to the dingy bar called Soldier's and stepped inside.

"ID?" the barkeep asked.

"Oh," Jeremy began, "I actually forgot—"

But the bartender cut him off, saying, "I'm just joking with you. There is no drinking age limit anymore, not when the world is about to end."

"Right," Jeremy replied slowly.

"So what will it be?" he asked, while polishing a glass.

"Um, just water, thanks."

"No water, here, pal. We only serve alcoholic beverages."

"How about just soda water and lime?" Jeremy asked.

"Sure. What do you have for it? We don't accept money here."

That's convenient, since I don't have any of that, Jeremy thought. He looked around the bar and saw there was a small weight scale, and near it a sign said:

Sugar: ten grams/drink

Salt: twenty grams/drink

Jeremy stopped reading at "salt." He rummaged around in his backpack until he found a package he'd been carrying all this time based on his mother's advice—salt was a useful preservative. She used to make her own prosciutto from ham for their family. Jeremy gave the man the ten grams of salt in exchange for the drink.

Jeremy sat in the corner of the bar, watching the carbon dioxide rise out of his glass. Out of the corner of his eye he saw the door open, and glancing up was dismayed to see it was not Dr. Miller, but a large tattooed biker. It took another three patrons to enter the bar before the distinctive white fluff of Dr. Miller's hair appeared. Dr. Miller went to the bar and ordered a pint of beer, immediately taking a big swig of the frothy drink.

Robert looked around and noticed Jeremy sitting by himself. He took a sip and walked over.

"You made it," Robert grunted as he sat down.

"It's nice to see you again, Dr. Miller!" Jeremy said, excited to start working, and to tell Dr. Miller about having seen the Ark.

Dr. Miller looked left and right and over his shoulder, before taking another long sip of his beer.

"Nice to see you too, Jeremy, but I don't have much time. I'm sorry it isn't under better circumstances, but I guess that's the way it is. We have been working for a few months in Los Alamos, New Mexico. It was actually where the first nuclear bomb was detonated, and the site of the Manhattan Project—I guess you learned that in school—but we moved back there to work on interstellar nuclear weapons against Shiva.

"A week ago, we got a severe increase in threats from some radical fundamentalist religious groups who believe that the coming apocalypse should not be stopped. The most influential of these people is a man named Matt Wilkinson, an evangelist preacher who has a lot of power in Washington. The Secretary of State, Robert Brighton, told me he thinks that there could be some people within our government hoping to dismantle our work in stopping the comet."

"They are trying to stop you from saving the world?" Jeremy asked incredulously.

"There are some who do not like the world. There are some who think it is flawed and that when they die, everything will be clear and perfect. Then there are the crazy people who just want to watch people burn."

Jeremy was confused about this, because to him it seemed like they should all want to save the planet. "Which ones are you most scared of?" Jeremy asked.

"I'm not sure, but I know that the Secretary of State is moving us to some island in the U.S. Virgin Islands to protect us while we work. I leave in a few days, but a lot of operations will continue from Johnson Space Center. I'm going to employ you as my research assistant. There are some things I need you to get from my office at the JSC, and above all I want to have someone I can trust there, outside of the traditional methods of communication."

"You think the people at the Johnson Space Center might try to sabotage the project?"

"It's possible. I need someone there I can trust. Can you do it?"

"Of course!"

Dr. Miller looked around before asking, "And where is Anna?"

Jeremy looked up and answered in a detached tone, "She stayed up in Colorado."

"Oh, alright."

"It's okay . . . I don't know. Anyways, who's the person I should be looking out for again?"

"His name is Matt Wilkinson, who the Secretary of Defense put in charge of the JSC. I just want you to be able to get an idea about what he's up to over there and anything out of the ordinary."

"Is he working with anyone, like an organization? Maybe the Union Anarchists?"

"The Union—oh no. Not them. These guys are

different. They started with death threats via email, saying that I was not allowed to play God."

"They are going to kill you?"

"I have no idea. They are getting crazy though, these fundamentalists."

Jeremy looked around the bar, seeing a lot of faces. It was only around three in the afternoon, but the dingy bar was crowded. Robert had almost finished his beer.

Jeremy sipped at his go-to drink at the bar: soda water and lime.

Now that Jeremy got a good view of Dr. Miller, he noticed how much older he looked than the last time he had seen him. The expression on his face exuded tiredness. Robert went into his front shirt pocket and pulled out a necklace. It had a wooden cross on it.

"Wear this. It might make you trustworthy, and will keep you out of trouble on the streets of Houston. Maybe learn a Bible verse or two."

"Do you know any?"

Robert considered for a minute, before replying:

"Proverbs 4:13 'The wise lay up knowledge, but the mouth of a fool brings ruin near.' I figure it's appropriate for now."

Jeremy laughed. *I think I'll pick a more 'I love Jesus'-style verse*, he thought.

Robert pulled out a sleek black phone from his pocket and gave it to Jeremy.

"Here, this cell phone runs on the government channels. It'll work, and behind it, in the credit card flap, is a ration card. With it, the United States will provide you with food and gasoline, and other essentials from the address on the card, on a weekly basis. Technically you're working for the United States government, so welcome aboard the machine. Oh! Also, there are some documents and things from my old office that I would like you to send via email to my new address, since not everything is digitized yet, so you'll have some non-spy things to do, too."

"Dr. Miller?"

"Yes?"

"Do you think there is a chance for the world?"

Dr. Miller looked into his beer glass. "I don't know," he said. "We will know a lot more as the comet comes closer to Earth. I'm sorry I don't have more time, Jeremy, but I have to go. Good luck with everything."

The two said goodbye then, and Jeremy left feeling motivated in a way he hadn't felt in his whole life. He was going to help save the world—or at least he would try!

12

ABYSS

December 1, 2016
Houston

Robert looked at Secretary Brighton and the Secret Service agents around them, navigating their group safely to their new home. They were to fly into Charlotte Amalie, the capital of the island of Saint Thomas in the U.S. Virgin Islands, using two planes. The thick Houston air left Robert sweating in the sweltering heat. He called Suri to wish her a good trip.

She sounded hassled. "Eight days to our next IMP deployment, and they need to move us now? I don't know if they could have chosen a worse time."

"Yeah, it's true, but the flight isn't long and we'll work on the way."

Robert's plane was the first to go. He got in and strapped himself to the seat, pulling out his computer and beginning to work. The nuclear weapons were ready for launch at Cape Canaveral and Vandenberg Air Force Base. There were ones at airstrips in South Dakota and in Russia as well. They were ready.

Before long, Robert was in the sky and working away. He landed in the heart-attack humidity of the U.S. Virgin Islands, and Robert seriously regretted leaving the cool tranquility of the New Mexico hills. *There was a reason Oppenheimer chose that place to work,* he thought. Robert started sweating within minutes of the plane landing.

Suri was slated to arrive in three days. Gerald was in constant contact with Robert as they discussed launch specifications as well as the integration with the nuclear weapons to the Vishnu spacecraft.

Once on the ground in Charlotte Amalie, Robert went to check into his hotel that the government had rented for them. Robert felt a little nervous about it becoming like a dorm. During his time in college his dorm life had caused much anxiety.

Robert was actually impressed by how most of the people he saw on the island seemed not to mind that the world was possibly going to end. He asked one of the hotel workers what they thought about the world ending.

"Hey, if it happens, it happens. Not much I will be able to do about it. But save us if you can," he said.

It made Robert laugh, and actually motivated him to work harder. He went into his hotel room and plopped down on the bed, taking a brief break. The next minute, he was fast asleep.

Three days later, Suri was working incessantly in her temporary office at the Johnson Space Center to get ready for her relocation to the island. She had not been able to reach her parents, but decided that she would see them again when, not *if*, she saved the world. In fact, she was working on a personal project—a sort of programming test—that might help with this. She didn't want to talk to Robert about it yet, as it wasn't finished. Suri knew that Robert would only call her a perfectionist for waiting, but she didn't care because she knew that for her project to work, it *had* to be perfect.

And she had to be watchful. Robert had told her that their security might be in danger at the Johnson Space Center, so she couldn't be sure eyes wouldn't be watching her. Many of the engineers she and Robert had hired were already on St. Thomas, so she didn't know if the new engineers at JSC were just new faces or were somehow untrustworthy. Finally, she packed her bags and headed to the airport, ready to be reunited with the teams fighting the comet.

• • •

Robert got a call on his cell phone, and since Suri was the only person who called him regularly, he immediately addressed her.

"Hey, Suri, you've landed then? Did you finish the compositions of—"

"Dr. Miller, this is Secret Service Agent Daniels," said a man with a deep, masculine voice. "I'm sorry to be the one to tell you this, sir, but there was an attack. The plane carrying the rest of your team was attacked . . . "

"What do you mean the plane attacked?"

"I'm sorry, sir. It happened before takeoff. We have two suspects in the bombing of the plane . . . "

But while Agent Daniels spoke to Robert, his mind would not take in more information.

"What?" he said again. "What happened to Suri? Suri Ladhka, the other scientists on board? Dr. Petrov? Where are they?"

"We do not have a body count yet, sir, but so far we have found no survivors. The detonation occurred near the fuel hull, sir . . . There . . . "

Robert couldn't hear the agent speaking on the phone. *No survivors*, he thought. *No survivors*. He held on to the *yet*.

"Robert?" Dr. Campero asked, from the other side of the hotel door. "Is everything all right?"